52181 $1.50

Don't believe everything you read. . . .

Dana suddenly jumped up and ran to the wastebasket, from which she plucked the crumpled issue of *NEWS2US*. "Oh, I've wanted to see this, but I just haven't been able to find a copy *anywhere*." Dana smoothed down the cover. "It was all sold out. I guess this was a popular issue."

"Look, Dana, I've already read the article. If you want the magazine, take it with you."

Dana turned the pages of the magazine as if she hadn't heard a word that Tom had said. "Wow, they sure make a good-looking couple, don't they?" She held the magazine out at arm's length so that Tom was forced to look at the picture. "They really look as if they belong together. They're both so blond and blue-eyed." Dana made *blond* and *blue-eyed* sound like *boring* and *dull*. "Of course *some* people would say that *we* make a stunning couple too, Tom. We're both so dark and mysterious looking." Dana ran a hand playfully through Tom's hair.

Tom hardly noticed. He was completely fixated on the picture. *Dana's right. They do look like the perfect couple. Did we ever look that right together?*

D0018959

Bantam Books in the Sweet Valley University series.
Ask your bookseller for the books you have missed.

And don't miss these Sweet Valley University Thriller Editions:

Visit the Official Sweet Valley Web Site on the Internet at:

http://www.sweetvalley.com

SWEET VALLEY UNIVERSITY®

Have You Heard About Elizabeth?

Written by
Laurie John

Created by
FRANCINE PASCAL

BANTAM BOOKS
NEW YORK · TORONTO · LONDON · SYDNEY · AUCKLAND

RL 8, age 14 and up

HAVE YOU HEARD ABOUT ELIZABETH?
A Bantam Book / February 1998

Sweet Valley High® and Sweet Valley University®
are registered trademarks of Francine Pascal.
Conceived by Francine Pascal.
Produced by Daniel Weiss Associates, Inc.
33 West 17th Street
New York, NY 10011.

All rights reserved.
Copyright © 1998 by Francine Pascal.
Cover art copyright © 1998 by Daniel Weiss Associates, Inc.
No part of this book may be reproduced or transmitted
in any form or by any means, electronic or mechanical,
including photocopying, recording, or by any information
storage and retrieval system, without permission in
writing from the publisher.
For information address: Bantam Books.

If you purchased this book without a cover you should be aware
that this book is stolen property. It was reported as "unsold and
destroyed" to the publisher and neither the author nor the pub-
lisher has received any payment for this "stripped book."

ISBN: 0-553-49220-9

Published simultaneously in the United States and Canada

Bantam Books are published by Bantam Books, a division of Bantam
Doubleday Dell Publishing Group, Inc. Its trademark, consisting of the
words "Bantam Books" and the portrayal of a rooster, is Registered in
U.S. Patent and Trademark Office and in other countries. Marca
Registrada. Bantam Books, 1540 Broadway, New York, New York 10036.

PRINTED IN THE UNITED STATES OF AMERICA

OPM   0 9 8 7 6 5 4 3 2 1

To Merry and Mort Young

Chapter One

"This is so wild!" Jessica Wakefield exclaimed as she flipped through the glossy pages of *NEWS2US*. With a luxurious sigh she leaned back against the pillows of her twin sister, Elizabeth's, neatly made bed and stretched her long slim legs out in front of her.

"Jess, do you think you could move over a little bit?" Elizabeth asked, shifting awkwardly on top of her pink-and-white-striped bedding.

"*Sorry*, Liz. I was just trying to get comfortable." Jessica would have preferred to stretch out on her own, much cozier bed with its lush purple satin comforter, but she didn't feel like moving the mound of beauty products, magazines, unopened textbooks, and weeks' worth of laundry that was piled high on top of it. "Hey, did you check out this article?"

"You mean the one about the rights of Chilean grape pickers?" Elizabeth asked.

1

"Excuse me? 'The Rights of Chilean Grape Pickers'? Are they a new band or something? I've never heard of them. Anyway, I was talking about *this*." Jessica held the magazine wide-open to show her sister a two-page, sultry photo layout titled "Hollywood's Five Hottest Leading Men Under Thirty."

"I mean, this magazine is *beyond* hip, Liz!" Jessica continued. "I can't *believe* that the next issue is going to feature *you!* Just think, in only a few more days the whole *world* will be reading about Elizabeth Wakefield, America's Most Fabulous Young Journalist!"

Jessica stopped turning the pages as an ad for self-tanner caught her eye. *Hmmm . . . maybe I should get some of that,* she thought distractedly. *I've been looking a little pale lately. But this model looks just* awful, *as if she hasn't waxed her legs in* days. . . .

"The article isn't going to just feature me, Jess," Elizabeth insisted. "Scott Sinclair's going to be featured too. And I'm not 'America's Most Fabulous Young Journalist!' The magazine is doing a whole series on 'fabulous young journalists' on campuses across America. Scott and I are just two of the people who got picked, that's all."

Some of these guys are pretty cute, Jessica realized as she turned to the photo essay on grape pickers. *Look at the shoulders on* that *one! Mmm-mm.*

"We were lucky, I guess," Elizabeth continued

as she stood up and casually walked over to her dresser. She picked up her brush and ran it through her long blond hair as if being written up in a national magazine happened to her every day.

That's just like Elizabeth, Jessica thought as she closed the magazine and tossed it on the floor. *Something totally cool happens, and she downplays it. If I were the one being interviewed, I'd take out a billboard and announce it to the world! Plus I'd make sure to wear something* fabulous *to the photo shoot,* Jessica concluded as she eyed her sister's outfit.

Although the Wakefield twins were identical in appearance, with sparkling aqua eyes and perfect size-six figures, the similarities ended there. Elizabeth was hardworking and studious, while Jessica was more fun loving and impulsive. Naturally their wardrobes tended to reflect their personalities. Jessica dressed to make the most of her tanned, California-girl good looks.

Comparing her own outfit to her sister's, Jessica couldn't help but smile. Jessica's turquoise halter top showed off her tan to perfection, and her white boy-cut shorts emphasized her slim waist and shapely legs. In contrast, while Elizabeth looked trim and athletic in her pressed chinos and lavender polo shirt, her clothes did nothing for her figure. Still, Elizabeth's fashion sense was hers and hers alone, and Jessica knew all too well there wasn't a thing she could do about it.

"It wasn't luck that got you and Scott picked for that article," Jessica said as she headed to the tiny kitchenette and selected a couple of cans of diet soda from their small refrigerator. "I'd say that scooping the scandal at the Verona Springs Country Club had something to do with it . . . not that you could have done it without *me*, of course." Jessica grinned, her eyes twinkling as she tossed Elizabeth a can of soda. "Or should I say, 'If not *para mí*, the whole, how do you say, *enterprise* would not have been *poh*-si-*blay*, *dahling!*'"

Jessica had had the time of her life when she and her boyfriend, Nick Fox, a police detective, had gone undercover to infiltrate the Verona Springs Country Club just a short couple of weeks earlier. Jessica had been begging Nick to take her on an assignment, and she'd even stumbled into a couple of Nick's dangerous sting operations along the way.

Nick hadn't been too keen on the idea of taking Jessica along, but he gave in when Jessica proved herself to be a mistress of disguise. Jessica created a fabulous "cover"—Perdita del Mar, a snooty, rich Argentinean heiress. Jessica had played her part to the hilt, dying her hair black and doing her best imitation of Madonna in the movie *Evita*. Not even her best friend, Lila Fowler, had been able to penetrate her disguise—not for a while anyway.

Jessica and Nick's undercover work, along with the efforts of Elizabeth, her sort-of boyfriend, Scott Sinclair, and her definitely ex-boyfriend Tom Watts had helped to expose an extortion racket at the heart of the ritzy club. Congressman Krandall's son Paul had been the ringleader, exploiting illegal aliens for slave labor by promising them working papers. Even Bruce Patman had ended up helping when he conked out Paul Krandall's partner in crime just after he'd held a gun on Tom Watts.

"I thought Perdita retired." Elizabeth put down her brush and popped open her soda. "At least I *hoped* she did."

"*Retired?*" Jessica shrieked. "Are you *crazy?* That act was award winning! Where would you be now if not for Perdita?"

Elizabeth smiled sadly but didn't answer. Chances were she wasn't thinking about what might have happened to *her* but to her jerky Tom Watts. Tom had sure come close to biting the dust. *Honestly,* Jessica thought. *Can she just forget about the past and think in the present tense for once?*

With that thought Jessica was reminded that going undercover had had its downside—in a big way. The excitement of the past couple of weeks didn't leave her much time for studying. It wasn't as if that was a major concern for Jessica in the first place, but she had missed a *major* exam in her creative-writing class. Jessica sighed in apprehension as she thought of her upcoming appointment with Professor Phinney.

It's so unfair, Jessica mused. Elizabeth *gets to be* interviewed *for her part in the country club scandal, and I have to convince a professor not to* flunk *me!* She paced restlessly around the room, eyeing her messy bed with longing. *Why can't I just snuggle up with my satin comforter and dream of Nick instead?* she wondered, a wicked smile growing on her face. *Hey, nothing's stopping me!*

With a flourish Jessica dumped half of the clutter on the floor and flopped down, collapsing against a mountain of fluffy pillows. But before she could relax, she was jabbed in the back by something pointy and unyielding.

"Ouch!" Jessica sat bolt upright, clutching the offending object: the broken-off heel of a gold evening shoe. *So* that's *where you were hiding,* she told the heel silently. *I've been looking all over for you! Now if I can just find the* rest of the shoe . . .

"Is something wrong, Jess?" Elizabeth looked at her quizzically as she twisted her silky hair into a ponytail.

"It's just not fair that *I* don't get any credit for helping crack the case," Jessica whined. "I mean, Professor Phinney is *totally* freaked that I missed his exam. Puh-*leeze!* As if what I was doing wasn't much more important!"

"You're right," Elizabeth agreed, her sea-colored eyes thoughtful. "Scott and I couldn't have done it without you *and* Nick *and* everybody else. I'll make sure that whoever interviews us knows that." She started applying the barest hint of lip gloss and mascara to her fresh-scrubbed face. "But don't worry about Professor Phinney, Jess. From what I hear, he's pretty sympathetic. Just tell him what happened, and I'm sure he'll give you a makeup exam."

"I'm not worried about *that*." Jessica waved a perfectly manicured hand dismissively. "But I'm supposed to meet him in twenty minutes—and that means I can't go shopping with the Thetas!"

Elizabeth smiled as she grabbed a flowered baseball cap from her top drawer. "Gee, Jess, I don't know. . . . Somehow that doesn't sound so terrible."

"You don't get it, Liz! My photo shoot with Bobby Hornet is only a few days away. I need to check out the latest innovations in bikini construction."

While her sister continued looking unimpressed, Jessica thought back to how desperately she'd wanted to be chosen to represent her sorority, Theta Alpha Theta, in the charity bikini calendar that would feature one of her favorite singers, Bobby Hornet. She'd practically knocked Bobby's eyes out when she'd worn nothing but a red bikini and matching spike heels to his appearance at Disc-Oh! Music; she'd reluctantly accepted a date with him; she'd even survived being found out by

Nick. But after all the thrills and excitement of undercover work, modeling hardly seemed to be a challenge. Finding the perfect bikini, however, was another matter.

Let's see, Jessica thought, mentally reviewing her current swimwear wardrobe. *The pink polka dot is too cutesy, the elastic in the purple is shot, and I need a darker tan to get away with the leopard skin.* . . . "Oh no, Liz! I *desperately* need some new bikinis!"

"Well, in that case, I *totally* feel your pain," Elizabeth said with a teasing smile..

"This isn't a joke, Liz. Bobby Hornet *personally* chose me for the cover shot *and* the December spread! Don't you realize what an honor that is? I mean, how often do *I* get to pose in a swimsuit calendar next to a famous rock star? I don't want to blow it by wearing some bikini that's totally passé!"

After all, I've been so busy riding sidesaddle with Nick lately, I haven't devoted nearly as much time as I should to my beauty routine. Jessica grimaced as she looked at her split ends. *I never had damaged hair before I went and trashed it by dying it black! Oh, well, at least my eyebrows have grown back. But I better show up in a to-die-for bikini or else.* . . .

"Sorry, Jess. I forgot how much this meant to you." Elizabeth looked contrite as she stood up and grabbed her leather backpack.

"Well, it's for a good cause," Jessica said, trying

to justify the project. "Bobby's donating all the proceeds to a homeless shelter. That's just as important as the rights of Chilean apple pickers."

"Grape pickers."

"Whatever."

Elizabeth laughed as she bent to give her sister a hug. "I've got to run. Good luck with Professor Phinney."

"Easy for you to say. You're not bikini deprived."

"Cheer up, Jess. Missing one Theta shopping session does *not* signal the end of the world. Besides, you already own quite a few bikinis."

Jessica pulled away from her sister in shock. "Elizabeth! I only have twelve! And some of them are *six months old!*"

Elizabeth smiled. "I'm sure you'll think of something." She headed out of the room, closing the door behind her with a calm *click*.

Doesn't Elizabeth get how freaked I am? Jessica wondered. *What if Professor Phinney fails me? What if I can't find the perfect bikini in time for the shoot? Or worse . . . what if my hair goes flat that day?*

Jessica fell back against the pillows, her face ashen.

Elizabeth dropped her backpack on her desk chair at the *Sweet Valley Gazette* and searched around for a sign of Scott Sinclair. *To an outsider the place probably looks like total chaos,* Elizabeth thought as interns rushed back and forth, trying to get the late edition under way. Ed Greyson, the editor in chief, was barking orders to a group of second-string reporters who were frantically taking notes, and the photo editor rushed by with a stack of still-dripping prints.

Even though I've only been here a little while, it already feels like home, Elizabeth thought with a satisfied smile. Before she joined the *Gazette* staff, she'd been working at WSVU, the campus television station. *I loved working there,* she mused, taking off her baseball cap and putting it in the top drawer of the desk she shared with Scott Sinclair. *Even though Scott puts television news down, there are some great things about the medium. Still, I couldn't stomach the thought of facing Tom every day. Not after we crashed and burned . . .*

Elizabeth's normally sunny expression clouded over as she remembered her painful breakup with Tom Watts, WSVU's station chief and the man she'd once considered the love of her life. It hadn't been so long ago that Elizabeth and Tom had been one of SVU's most golden couples, known across campus for their hard-hitting investigative reports.

But we weren't just a great news *team,* she reminded herself with a wince. *We were a great team,* period. *I thought we were indestructible, but that was before George Conroy entered the picture.* Elizabeth closed her eyes briefly, trying in vain to block out the memories that threatened to flash before her.

Tom's entire family had been killed in a car crash his freshman year, so it had been a shock to him to discover that the man he had grown up with all those years wasn't his real father and that his biological father, George Conroy, was very much alive.

It meant so much for Tom to have a family again—and I was happy for him too! Elizabeth recalled. *Everything was going so well. Why did Mr. Conroy have to come on to me? Why didn't Tom believe me when I told him? Why—*

"Hey, Liz, over here!"

Her traumatic flashback receding, Elizabeth turned and saw Scott Sinclair waving to her from the doorway of the glass-enclosed conference room. Behind him stood a photographer who was loading his camera and a woman using a cell phone. *Those must be the people from* NEWS2US, Elizabeth realized with a small pang of anxious excitement.

As Elizabeth made her way through the maze of desks, she couldn't help but admire Scott's wholesomely handsome face. With his chin-length, sun-streaked blond hair and crystal clear blue eyes that sparkled with intelligence, Scott looked like the perfect cross between a model and an honor student. But even more noticeable than his spectacular good looks was the aura of total confidence he projected. Particularly now, as he stood in the midst of the teeming *Gazette* offices, his calm self-assurance made him stand out from the rest of the staff like a movie star.

"Elizabeth, I'd like you to meet Christine Elliot, the reporter from *NEWS2US,* and Kurt Morris, the photographer," Scott announced smoothly. "Christine, Kurt, this is my partner in crime, Elizabeth Wakefield." He draped his arm around Elizabeth's shoulders and gave her a friendly squeeze.

Elizabeth hoped her blush was imperceptible. Back when they were investigating the Verona Springs Country Club, she and Scott had had to pretend that they were a couple. Somewhere along the way the lines between make-believe and reality had become blurred. Even though Elizabeth didn't think she was ready for a new romance, she and Scott had fallen into one—an uncomfortable, tentative one.

As Elizabeth disengaged herself from Scott's arm she couldn't help but think she would've been less quick to remove herself from Tom Watts's clasp. *Tom's arm would have felt more . . . supportive,* she reasoned. *Somehow Scott just makes me feel more nervous.* Elizabeth swallowed, trying to quell the slight case of butterflies she was experiencing.

"Nice to meet you, Ms. Wakefield," Christine Elliot said. Christine's handshake was brisk and efficient, her hair was pulled back in a no-non-sense bun, and she wore a businesslike beige suit. Kurt Morris seemed more laid-back—his hair was caught back in a ponytail with a leather thong, and he was wearing jeans and sandals. He didn't shake Elizabeth's hand but merely nodded at her as he busied himself with a light meter.

"It's nice to meet you too." Elizabeth laughed. "Actually that's an understatement—it isn't every day that I get to be interviewed by a national newsmagazine!" On hearing her own words, Elizabeth was briefly overcome with awe at the realization that hundreds of thousands—maybe even *millions*—of people would be reading about her next week.

Scott smiled at Christine, who was efficiently setting up her tape recorder. "Liz and I are usually on your side of the microphone," he remarked. "This is kind of new for us."

"I guess now you'll get to see how the other half lives," Christine joked. She finished assembling her equipment and tilted the microphone toward Elizabeth. "So, Ms. Wakefield, can you tell me how you and Mr. Sinclair were able to uncover the Krandall Scandal at Verona Springs?" she asked suddenly.

"Well . . . um, it was really a group effort," Elizabeth replied modestly, caught off guard. "So many people at SVU helped. My sister, Jessica; her boyfriend, Nick Fox . . ."

13

Elizabeth trailed off for a moment as Tom Watts's name hovered on the tip of her tongue. Should she mention Tom? She had to admit it was only fair. No matter what had gone on between them, he *had* helped the investigation. She took a deep breath and continued. "Tom—"

"That's right," Scott interrupted. "Even though Elizabeth and I make a great duo, we weren't working alone. It was a team effort all the way."

Elizabeth nodded. Although she was slightly irritated that Scott had cut her off, she was glad that he was being generous about sharing the credit. "My sister actually went undercover in order to—"

"Could you guys move a little to the left?" Kurt demanded, frowning as he adjusted his light meter. "The light isn't strong enough over here. See if you can edge over by the window. I know there's not a lot of room with that desk in the way, but we don't have much choice."

Elizabeth and Scott dutifully moved over. It was a tight squeeze. Elizabeth was pretty uncomfortable, but they were jammed so closely together, she couldn't make any adjustments. *If this is how the other half lives, I'll be more sympathetic the next time I conduct an interview,* Elizabeth thought. *I wouldn't want to force my subject into such an awkward position!*

"How did it feel to uncover such a major story? After all, this was no run-of-the-mill country club affair. The two of you were responsible for indicting Congressman Krandall's son on multiple charges— murder as well as extortion." Christine paused and looked expectantly at Elizabeth.

Elizabeth was too dazed by the sudden flash of Kurt's camera to answer. She blinked several times and nearly lost her balance as Scott reached out a protective arm to steady her.

"Both of us feel that the press is an instrument for justice. Its purpose is to inform the public," Scott replied. "Our goal wasn't to bring down a congressman's son; it was simply to discover who was responsible for the terrible things that had been happening at Verona Springs. As it turned out, we got in the way of some pretty big people."

Elizabeth couldn't help but be impressed by the way Scott was handling things. *He sounds as if he's been answering questions like these for years,* she mused. *He hardly seems bothered by the fact that we're crammed in this corner like sardines, being blinded by flashes. I'm not handling this half as smoothly as he is!* Elizabeth wondered if Christine was thinking the same thing. Her fears appeared to be confirmed when she noticed that the reporter had turned to focus all her attention on Scott.

"What's up next?" Christine continued. "Are you following any hot leads now?"

"Sorry, Christine, but *we* can't tell you that," Scott said with a laugh.

Elizabeth pushed aside her fears, relieved that

Scott was taking the question for both of them. She needed a bit of breathing space while she gathered her thoughts.

"After all," Scott continued, "we wouldn't want you to scoop us, would we?"

"That would be pretty hard, from what I can tell. You seem like an ace reporter. I'm sure I could learn a few tricks from you!"

After sharing a long laugh with Scott, Christine turned to face Elizabeth. "Well, what about you? Do you agree with Scott about the purpose of journalism? What are your future plans? I'm sure that our readers would want to know."

"I believe that investigative reporting can be a powerful tool for change," Elizabeth said, her voice growing in confidence as she continued. "Look at the way the world reacted when the press made clear what was happening in Bosnia. A war crimes tribunal was set up. Would that have happened if a group of courageous journalists hadn't told the story? That's what a good reporter can accomplish. I like to think that I'm a good enough reporter to effect that kind of change."

Elizabeth paused and took a deep breath. *I'm glad I finally got to say something substantial, but was it substantial enough?* she wondered. *After all, NEWS2US is a major periodical. A good quote in there could help me get into the Denver Center for Investigative Reporting!*

Not long after the Verona Springs story broke, Scott had sent in an application to DCIR, a prestigious journalism school, and had urged and convinced Elizabeth to do the same. The more she thought about it, the less she was sure she wanted to leave SVU. But she figured it wouldn't hurt her to at least apply, and if they accepted her, well, who knew? *Perhaps if I give* NEWS2US *a few more choice quotes, the admissions department at DCIR will have even more reason to accept me,* Elizabeth thought, clearing her throat to get Christine's attention. "You know, Christine, I also think the press is responsible for—"

"Give me a big smile, Elizabeth," Kurt broke in.

Elizabeth sighed in frustration at being interrupted yet again. But Scott flashed her a sympathetic grin, and Elizabeth returned it gratefully.

"That's good!" Kurt said. "Great smile! But there's a shadow on your face that I don't like. Can you look up at Scott a little more? There . . . that should take care of it."

Elizabeth smiled brightly as stars from the exploding flash danced before her eyes.

This has to be one of the most fabulous—and fabulously expensive—*boutiques I've ever been in!* Denise Waters thought with a sigh as she sank down in one of the ornate brocade chairs that were scattered throughout Chris and Candies, a chic clothing store that had recently opened in Sweet Valley.

"Is this wicked or *what?*" Lila Fowler shrieked, jarring Denise out of her reverie. She held up a black vinyl two-piece dress. "Bruce would die if I wore it!" Lila held the dress against herself and went to take a look in the full-length gilded mirror on the other side of the floor. She sucked in her cheeks as she turned from side to side in total self-admiration.

"Try it on," Isabella Ricci urged, her hammered copper bracelets jingling as she brushed a silky strand of raven hair away from her face.

"Are you *kidding?*" Lila sniffed. "It's just so . . . *plebeian.* And these cutouts along the sides are a little too obvious, don't you think? If it's got to be vinyl, it's got to be *elegant.*" Lila tossed the dress aside.

Denise looked at the discarded dress, gasping as she caught sight of the price tag. "It may not be elegant, but it certainly is expensive!"

Lila shrugged an aristocratic shoulder as she moved on to a basket overflowing with silk scarves.

How can this cost so much? Denise wondered. *It doesn't even have sleeves!* Denise got out of the chair and hung the dress back up. *I'm so out of my league here cashwise. Maybe I shouldn't have come along in the first place, even if it is my duty as a Theta.*

Morosely Denise followed Lila and Isabella over to the evening wear section. All of a sudden the one purchase she had allowed herself—a polka-dot cotton halter—seemed awfully shabby

18

compared to the silks and satins her sorority sisters were inspecting.

So what? she asked herself. *Stop feeling sorry for yourself. Everyone says that you've got a great sense of style. After all, would you have learned to be such a creative dresser if you had money to burn? No way!*

Denise and her boyfriend, Winston Egbert, were known for their thrift shop finds. Today Denise was wearing a forties-retro dress with a tiny yellow-and-white floral print. The bias cut showed off her slim figure to perfection.

Even Lila admires my taste! Denise noted as Lila lifted a similar forties-style dress from the racks. *Yeah, except Lila's holding a Paris original that costs a fortune and my dress has moth holes in it!* Denise couldn't help feeling wistful. Just once she longed to be able to walk into a store and buy everything she wanted. Just once . . .

"Now *this* is more like it," Lila exclaimed, pulling an exquisite evening dress off the rack. The bright lights from the overhead chandelier reflected off the sheer, silvery chiffon. The high neck and open back were truly stunning. "Is this to die for or what?" She ran her hands through the shimmering folds of the fabric, frowning as she held her crimson nails against it. "Izzy, do you still have that luscious lilac nail polish? That color would be *divine* with this!"

"I might have some left," Isabella replied as she

rifled through the selection of dresses. "I think Jessica used it the last time we had a Theta manicure session."

Denise ran her hands through the silks and satins hanging from the rack. "Mmm . . . these fabrics feel *glorious*. I never want to wear another rayon dress again!"

"This would look good on you, Denise. What do you think?" Isabella held up a dress for Denise's inspection.

Her blue eyes wide, Denise reached out to take the peach silken dress from Isabella. "What do I think? I think it might be worth spending the rest of my life in prison just to see the look on Winnie's face if I . . ." Trailing off, she pulled her hair back as she went to model the dress in front of the mirror. "What do you think, Izzy? Does this dress call for an up do? Or should I leave a few tendrils hanging down?"

"Prison?" Isabella raised a perfectly arched brow as she joined Denise at the mirror. "What on earth are you talking about?"

Denise laughed ruefully as she looked at the shocked expression on Isabella's face. "Oh, I'm really low on funds right now. I ran through most of my allowance, and I hate to ask my parents for more. Right now the only way I could get a dress like this is to steal it." She hung the dress back where it belonged with a sigh.

"Do you want to borrow some cash, Denise?"

Isabella reached into her fawn-colored Italian leather purse without even blinking.

Denise shook her head mournfully. "No, thanks. It's sweet of you to offer, though."

"Suit yourself." Isabella shrugged. "Anyway, I don't see what you're worried about. You *always* look great. You've got such a sense of—"

"Style. Yeah, I know." At the biting sound of her own voice she exhaled contritely. "Sorry, Izzy. I didn't mean to sound ungrateful. That's quite a compliment coming from you." Denise gestured at Isabella's clean-lined, coral linen dress. The contrast with her pale porcelain skin and raven hair was striking, and the hammered copper bracelets lent a funky edge to what would otherwise have been a ho-hum look.

"Hey, guys." Mandy Carmichael came over, balancing several heavy-looking packages. She dumped them unceremoniously on the floor and sank down gratefully into one of the brocade chairs. "Isn't anyone up for a drink?" She waved her hand toward the European-style espresso bar at the back of the store.

Lila, who had just come out of a dressing room clad in the silver dress, tossed her chestnut mane and stared at Mandy in amazement. "You want to take a *break*? I'm just getting started!"

"I'm with Mandy," Alexandra Rollins said, joining them. "I'm not going to make it back to campus without resting my feet *or* having an iced cappuccino."

Several other Thetas groaned in agreement.

Lila waved her hand dismissively. "You go on ahead. *We'll* join you when *we're* done." Lila turned her attention back to the mirror. "This would be perfect for dinner with Bruce on Friday," she murmured, pirouetting on one foot.

Bruce Patman, Lila's boyfriend, was one of the few people at SVU who was as rich as she was. Unlike most students, whose idea of a Friday night date was nachos and a video, Bruce and Lila only went to the most expensive restaurants and clubs. They'd even been members of the ultraexclusive Verona Springs Country Club before they'd resigned in disgust after the big scandal broke.

Denise sighed, imagining what she and Winston would most likely do on Friday: watch TV in the Oakley dorm lounge and order in a pizza, fighting down to the last penny over who owed what. *It must be nice to go to gourmet restaurants all the time the way Lila and Bruce do,* Denise thought with a twinge of jealousy. *When will Winnie and I be able to afford things like that?*

"I should get something for Bruce too," Lila continued, returning to the dressing room. "He hasn't gotten any new clothes in *weeks*."

"Poor thing!" Denise choked back a giggle.

Lila shot Denise a look as she came out with the dress tucked securely under her arm. But she didn't say anything as she dragged Denise over to the men's side of the store.

As she sifted through the cashmere sweaters and silk ties, Denise felt another pang. *I'd like to buy something for Winnie too,* she thought wistfully. *It would be nice to see him in cashmere instead of flannel for once.*

"This might be nice on Bruce." Denise held out a red-and-blue-striped tie for Lila's inspection.

"That's so investment banker!" Lila said disdainfully. "This, however, would look *divine* on Bruce." Lila selected a sea-foam-colored raw silk shirt and casually added several sweaters to her ever growing pile of merchandise. "C'mon—I'm ready for that iced cappuccino now if you are." Lila led the way to the register and tossed down her gold card.

A cappuccino. Now there's one thing I can afford, Denise thought. *Oh, well, one day I'll have enough money to buy everything I want. Yeah, and by then I'll be so old, the only thing I'll want will be a wheelchair!*

Chapter Two

". . . So you see, Professor Phinney—even though I missed the exam, I *was* actually involved in a creative-writing project. After all, I needed to create a script in order to 'flesh out' the character of Perdita, my undercover identity."

Professor Phinney arched his eyebrows silently.

"Well, maybe I didn't write it *down,* exactly, but I *thought* about it. . . ."

Jessica gave her professor her most winning smile as she sat back in the hardwood chair reserved for his office visitors. The rest of Professor Phinney's office was decorated like a library on an English country estate, with leather chairs and a deep red-and-gold Persian carpet. Oak bookcases lined the walls from floor to ceiling, their shelves groaning under the weight of several hundred rare volumes bound in crimson leather. Jessica felt slightly awed by the surroundings, but Professor

Phinney looked perfectly at home in his tweed jacket and school tie. As he played with a collection of antique fountain pens on his desk, he shot Jessica a stern look.

"I see. . . . Ah, what *exactly* did you say you accomplished as a result of going undercover?" The professor picked up a brass paperweight and turned it over in his hands, studying it as if it contained the secrets of the universe.

Hasn't he even been listening to a word I've said? Jessica wondered. *I mean,* c'mon, *as if my story isn't a lot more interesting than some paperweight! Well, I've got to prove it to him . . . or else he'll flunk me!*

Jessica took a deep breath to calm herself and started again. "My boyfriend, Nick—Nick Fox—is a cop," she began. *And he's also the best boyfriend in the world!* Jessica couldn't help saying to herself. Just the thought of him made her confidence grow by degrees.

"He'd just gotten a new assignment to go undercover at the Verona Springs Country Club," she continued. "You see, one of the caddies had been murdered, and Nick's captain thought that the club needed some in-depth investigating. Nick wouldn't even *think* of going undercover without me."

Well, he wouldn't have thought about it at all if I hadn't threatened to break up with him! Jessica giggled as she remembered the screaming fit she'd had in front of Nick's colleagues at the police station. *Besides, Chief Wallace wanted me to go, so*

25

Nick didn't even have a choice. Ha! I showed him, all right.

"Everybody knows that I'm a master of disguise," she continued. "Nick was a little concerned about my safety, but I would *never* let a little thing like that get in the way of truth, justice, and . . . and all that stuff." Jessica stole a glance at Professor Phinney to see if he was paying any attention. He appeared to have his eyes closed. She sighed deeply but soldiered on.

"So anyway, I created this totally fabulous character, Perdita del Mar. I mean, she just had the best fash—um, the best *criminal* instinct. It wasn't all fun and games either. I sacrificed quite a bit! I dyed my hai—uh, I had to stay up all night on several round-the-clock stakeouts. Yeah . . . *yeah!* About a dozen highly sensitive, life-threatening, round-the-clock stakeouts."

When Jessica paused to gather momentum, she noticed that Professor Phinney had opened his eyes and was giving her a skeptical look. *Well, at least I know he's listening!* Jessica thought, leaning forward with excitement. Her eyes sparkled as she gripped the sides of her chair. *This story is even getting to* me. *Now just wait until he hears the rest of this!*

Clearing her throat, she blasted full speed ahead. "We'd been pretty successful at infiltrating the club, but the investigation was at a standstill. Nobody could figure out who was behind all the shady goings-on."

Yeah, well, I had a pretty good idea that it would turn out to be Paul Krandall. . . . Any guy who'd date a girl like Bunny Sterling would have to be suspect, right? I mean, ugh! Those teeth!

"Nobody but me, of course." Jessica tossed her long blond hair over her shoulder. "I mean, I suspected Paul Krandall from the beginning. Call it instinct, call it a hunch . . . but I had to make sure. I couldn't send an innocent man off to jail for life . . . oh no. I couldn't have that on my, uh, *consciousness.*" *This is it,* she told herself. *It's all or nothing. Give it all you got!*

"So using my antiencryption device, I hacked into the FBI's computers."

Encryption is a word, isn't it? Or is it kryptonite? *Whatever!*

"Using skills I acquired in my high-school computer science course, I hacked into their files to see if their profile on Paul matched mine."

Well, I did join that detective film fan club chat group on the Internet. . . .

"When I saw what the bureau had on Paul, I knew I had my man." Jessica paused dramatically. "Now all I had to do was bring him in. But how?"

Um, yeah. How did I do that anyway?

"Uh, I figured the best way was to flirt with . . . um, was to dig an underground tunnel to the bungalow . . . yeah . . . the safe house where Paul was drink—um, hiding!" Jessica finished the sentence triumphantly.

Boy, am I glad I figured that one out! But what happened next? Think! Think!

"However, I didn't expect him to see right through my ruse and kidnap me! Luckily I was prepared. You see, it was part of my cover as Perdita to wear the most fabulous jewelry. I had on these absolutely gorgeous gold bracelets, and when Paul tied my wrists . . . voilà! I just slid my hands out of the bracelets. I was home free!"

Yeah, it's too bad I lost those, Jessica lamented. Paul should pay for them. I should remember to call his lawyer when I'm finished here . . . whoops! Gotta stick to the story!

"Well, I wasn't quite home free because he'd kidnapped me in a big ugly cargo van, and we were going six . . . about a hund . . . about one hundred and fifty miles an hour. I mean, some of those old Volkswagens really book! Anyway, I threw myself out of the van onto the highway. . . ."

Come on, Jessica urged the professor silently. Aren't you buying any of it? This story rocks, and most of it's even true!

"And after I clawed my way out of the ditch, I flagged down Bruce Patman, who happened to be driving by in his Porsche. I didn't even care that I'd broken a nail or two. You see, when I'm on a case, there's no stopping me! So anyway, we followed the van, and when Paul got out, I knew I had him. I don't like to brag, but I'm a gold lamé—I mean, black belt in karate. I was schooled in a Shaolin temple, just like in that movie with the kung fu guy who only had one arm and—"

"I've heard enough, Miss Wakefield." Professor Phinney held up his hands to stop Jessica's flood of words. "I must say, I've never heard a more . . . *outlandish* story."

"You . . . you haven't?" Jessica moaned. Her stomach sank, and her face burned with embarrassment. *Oh no! He didn't go for it! I'm going to fail!*

"In fact," the professor continued, "even if I hadn't already decided to excuse you based on the report I'd seen on WSVU and the articles I'd read in the *Gazette,* I might feel compelled to do so now. But . . . anyone who can reel off a story that wildly inventive obviously deserves an A."

"What did you say?" Jessica blinked. "I deserve a . . . what?"

"An A, Ms. Wakefield."

Have I finally gone crazy? she wondered. *Am I hearing things? Is this some kind of freaky extension of my story?*

"I said, young lady, that your story was quite brilliant." Professor Phinney gave Jessica a wide smile. "Even if you hadn't just demonstrated your creative storytelling abilities, I would have still been impressed with your courage. I'm giving you an A."

Jessica suppressed the urge to do a victory dance. Suddenly Professor Phinney's office seemed brighter, as if it were lit by the glow of her own happiness. She couldn't remember the last time she'd gotten an A . . . or if she'd ever gotten one in her life to begin with.

"Thank you, Professor Phinney," Jessica gasped. She quickly gathered her books together and headed for the door, afraid that if she lingered one second longer, the professor might change his mind. "Thank you again, Professor. Really."

"It's my pleasure, Ms. Wakefield," Professor Phinney called as she headed out the door. "I look forward to hearing more of your stories in class."

Jessica danced out of the office with a dazzling smile on her face. *This is unbelievable!* she thought, a tingling sensation suffusing her whole body. She felt as if she'd just found an incredible Gaudicci dress on sale for eighty percent off. *No, better than that,* she told herself. *I just found the dress on sale* and *they threw in the perfect pair of shoes for free!*

Ignoring the stupefied looks of everyone around her, Jessica skipped across the quad. "Now I *know* I should pursue this law-and-order thing," she said aloud. "It's *awesome!*"

"So, did you guys get everything you need on Liz and me?" Scott asked casually. He reached for Elizabeth's hand and loosely clasped it.

"I think we covered it all," Christine said, glancing up from numbering the tapes she had made of the interview.

"In that case, we're out of here. We're going to grab some coffee at the Red Lion. OK, Liz?" Scott asked as he gently swung her hand back and forth.

Well, I'd love a coffee, Elizabeth replied silently, embarrassed that Scott would make such a childishly romantic gesture in front of an important journalist. *But I need a break from you!*

"Sorry, Scott." Elizabeth gave him a regretful smile that belied the irritation she was feeling inside. "I've got an exam on the other side of campus, and I barely have time to make it." Elizabeth hated to lie; her exam had been yesterday. But after that grueling interview she needed some breathing space desperately.

Elizabeth shifted her gaze away from Scott's, worried that her face might reveal her lie. *Why is it that Scott just assumes I'll go along with his plans sometimes?* she wondered gloomily. *Doesn't he realize that I don't feel comfortable with this—whatever this is—yet?*

Elizabeth turned toward Christine and Kurt. "Thanks for interviewing us. It was really an honor."

"Yeah, it was great," Scott chimed in. "Listen, I'm going to walk Elizabeth out, but I'll be back in a second if you guys want to hang," he said with easy charm as he held the glass conference-room door open for Elizabeth.

"How do you think we did?" Elizabeth asked once they were out of earshot. She retrieved her baseball cap from her desk drawer and put it on squarely. "Do you think it went OK?"

Scott tweaked the bright blond ponytail that peeked out from the back of Elizabeth's cap. "I think it was fine," he said with a small smile. He leaned forward—very slowly—and kissed Elizabeth's forehead softly.

Elizabeth closed her eyes for a second, letting the sweet sensation of Scott's touch wash over her. She relaxed against the warmth of his chest for a moment, feeling a gentle flutter in her heart as his hand stroked her back. *Sometimes things feel so right with Scott,* she thought, still savoring the sugar of his kiss. *But I still feel uncomfortable about getting involved with him.*

Sighing, Elizabeth shifted her position a little. A swirl of nervousness grew in her stomach as his arms tightened around her. *What's wrong with me?* she asked herself. *I must be crazy! Scott is handsome, brilliant, ambitious . . .*

. . . and he's not Tom Watts.

Elizabeth stifled a groan. *Face it,* a cruel voice inside her head taunted. *You're still hung up on Tom, and* that *relationship is yesterday's news!*

"I've . . . I've got to get going, Scott," Elizabeth insisted, disengaging from his embrace.

"Yeah. I'll catch you later," Scott said. Surprisingly his grin looked a bit less dazzling than usual.

Is it my imagination, or was he a little hurt? Elizabeth wondered as she left the *Gazette* offices

32

and started walking toward Dickenson Hall. The afternoon was brilliantly sunny, and the breeze was deliciously soft. Sunbathers dotted the lawn, and one enterprising couple had set up a barbecue. But Elizabeth was too deep in thought to notice any of these things as she strode purposefully across the quad, her hands jammed in her pockets.

"Maybe it's not too late to work things out with Tom," Elizabeth murmured, nervously chewing on her lip. "Maybe I'm *supposed* to work things out with him." She almost collided with a Frisbee in her path. Without even noticing what she was doing, she grabbed it and easily tossed it back to its owners.

Elizabeth shook her head slowly. "I can't be the only one who's hurting. He must *still* have some feelings for me." Elizabeth came to a standstill in the middle of the quad. "I just don't know what to do. I'm so confused."

I need some quality time with myself, she resolved with determination. *I am going to get a coffee—alone!—and I'm going to write in my journal until I can make some sense of my feelings.*

Turning on her heels, Elizabeth headed toward the coffee shop. The outdoor café, with its wrought iron tables and bright green-and-white-striped umbrellas, seemed like the perfect soothing spot to relax and clear her head.

"Why didn't I think of this before?" Elizabeth

chided herself. "All I need is a little private time with my journal, a little—"

Elizabeth's jaw dropped, and she stared in disbelief at the sight that greeted her eyes. "I—I don't believe it," she muttered, stopping dead in her tracks.

Even though she was still twenty yards from the coffee shop, there was no mistaking the pair of broad shoulders that rested against the curved, filigreed back of one of the café chairs. How many times had Elizabeth cried on those strong shoulders, been comforted by the muscular arms that were casually draped across the armrests?

Tom! She drew a deep breath. *Maybe this is an omen. Maybe I was* meant *to run into him now!*

Elizabeth swallowed hard, trying to gather the courage to approach him. But her heart plummeted as she caught a glimpse under the table, where a pair of Dr. Marten sandals seductively played footsie with Tom's high-tops. Her eyes followed the sandals up to a plaid, schoolgirl-style miniskirt and cotton blouse that would have been demure if it hadn't been skintight.

Dana Upshaw! Elizabeth realized, her heart ripping into pieces, her pulse loud and angry in her ears. *How could I be so stupid? Tom made his feelings clear when I ran into him last week.*

Her eyes blurring with tears, Elizabeth remembered that last time she'd talked to him—a stiff, seething confrontation that had resulted in Tom

34

walking away from her and Elizabeth stuffing her application to DCIR in the nearest mailbox. *I'd realized then that there was nothing left between us,* she told herself. *Tom's completely over me—and completely into Dana. Why can't I get the point?*

A burst of laughter jarred Elizabeth out of her reverie. She stood rooted to the spot as she watched Dana fling back her glossy mahogany mane and swoop forward to kiss Tom's cheek. Elizabeth felt her tears begin to fall.

"So what?" she said defiantly. "Who cares? Tom Watts isn't the *only* guy at SVU. I'm dating one of the best-looking men on this campus right now!"

I should have come here with Scott after all, she thought vengefully as she wiped her eyes. *I'd show Tom that I'm not pining over him! I'd kiss Scott right in front of him—and it wouldn't be just a peck on the cheek either!*

Deliberately averting her eyes from the spectacle Tom and Dana were making, she walked away from the café, never once looking back.

"Hey, hold on a sec! Take it easy!" Tom laughed as he pushed Dana Upshaw's caressing arms away. "Mary will be back any second," he said, looking around and spotting his ten-year-old half sister, who was busy getting an ice-cream cone.

"Mmmm," Dana moaned, seductively stroking his

forearm with the cool tip of a finger. "We wouldn't want to set a bad example, now, would we?"

Tom smiled in spite of the heat that was collecting under his collar. Public displays of affection always made him uncomfortable, but that never seemed to bother Dana. *I don't know why I'm so darned squeamish,* Tom thought, his eyes unconsciously wandering to where Dana's short plaid skirt left little to the imagination. *Most guys would kill to have a woman who looked . . . and dressed . . . and* acted *like this all over them!*

Dana sat back and took a dainty sip of her lemonade. As she lazily stirred the straw around in the old-fashioned red-and-white glass, her sandals played a different tempo with Tom's feet.

Why does she have to keep playing footsie? Tom asked himself. The first time Tom had felt her foot under the table, he'd thought a squirrel was attacking his shoelaces.

Dana finished her drink and made the pouting face that Tom had thought was adorable the first fifty times he'd seen it. It was wearing a little thin now, and sometimes Tom couldn't help wondering if he was only seeing Dana because of . . .

Elizabeth! Tom caught the flicker of a blond ponytail out of the corner of his eye. He twisted around in his seat so that he could get a better view. *Yup, that's her, all right. What's she in such a hurry for?* he wondered. *I know it can't have anything to do with me. She's probably rushing off to see her new boyfriend, Scott Slimeball—I mean, Sinclair.* His stomach lurched at the thought.

I guess Elizabeth wasn't hit too hard by our breakup after all, he mused. *She certainly seems to be going through a lot of guys these days. First Todd Wilkins, now Sinclair. Who's next on her list? The groundskeeper?*

Suddenly he felt a playful swat at his arm. "*To-*om! You're not *listening!*" Dana whined. "OK. So anyway, as I was saying, Anthony *really* feels that I've gotten a handle on the concerto. I was a little worried at first when it didn't seem to be coming together, but now I'm comfortable with the melodic understructure, which is totally great." Dana paused and looked at Tom expectantly. "Don't you agree? Tom?"

"What? Uh, yeah, Dana. That's . . . great." Tom wasn't exactly sure what he was agreeing with, but some sort of answer seemed to be called for. It must have been the right one because Dana nodded in apparent satisfaction and rambled on.

"The best part is that I might be able to play it with the SVU orchestra. That is, if everything goes according to plan. You see . . ."

While Dana continued talking, Tom recalled how he had been fascinated by her stories about the music world—at first. Dana was not only a cellist but was also Mary Conroy's cello tutor, which was how Tom had come to meet her in the first place.

She does *have a way of going on and on, doesn't she?* Tom thought, tuning out Dana completely as he swirled the remaining ice cubes at the bottom of his glass. *Well, so what if Dana is a little boring sometimes? So what if she only talks about herself? I'm not going to hang around my dorm room alone while Elizabeth dates half the men on this campus!*

"Tom!" Dana shrieked, causing him to start and spill the ice on his pants. "Haven't you been listening to a word I've been saying?" Her hazel eyes blazed as she crossed her arms over her chest and stared at him confrontationally.

"Of course, yeah, you were talking about the orchestra. . . ." Tom grabbed several napkins and started to dab at the wet spot.

"That was *ten minutes* ago. Honestly, Tom! Sometimes you just seem to be in another world." Dana glared at Tom for a moment before her face relaxed into a smile. "If I didn't know better, I'd say that you were immune to my charms," she murmured as she snuggled up against him. She took the napkins from Tom's hand and began to mop up the mess herself.

An uncontrollable blush crept up Tom's neck, but it subsided as little Mary trotted back to the table, ice-cream cone in hand. At least Dana had enough presence of mind to stop messing with Tom's pants.

Thank goodness for little half sisters, Tom thought.

"I couldn't decide between the chocolate chocolate chip and the mint chocolate chip, so I got both," Mary announced, her huge cone threatening to drip all over her perfectly starched pink dress.

"Are you sure your father wouldn't mind you eating that much ice cream, Mary?" Dana asked with playful concern. She reached into the huge leather tote that hung from her chair and fished out a turquoise-studded barrette. "Here. You don't want your hair to get in the ice cream," she said sweetly, pinning back Mary's long, curly blond hair.

"Thanks, Dana. Dad doesn't care how much ice cream I eat as long as I make sure to eat all my vegetables too." Mary made a face and giggled.

"That's what I call a really cool father!" Dana said, her musical laughter blending in with Mary's. She shot Tom a glance, as if expecting him to join in, but Tom remained stock silent. When it came to his father, George Conroy, there was nothing to laugh about.

Mary nodded enthusiastically. "Dad's the best. You think so too, Tom, don't you?" Suddenly her ice cream seemed forgotten as she turned to face Tom, her face puckered with concern. "You haven't been hanging around with us lately. Dad really misses you." She smiled shyly. "And me and Jake miss you too."

Tom reached out to ruffle Mary's hair. He was

touched by her affection, and he couldn't help feeling guilty. *I didn't mean to ignore Mary and Jake,* Tom thought, trying to remember the last time he'd seen his scruffy little half brother. *The last thing I want to do is hurt their feelings. They shouldn't have to suffer because of my problems with George.*

"Mary, I'm sorry that I haven't had a chance to come over lately," Tom said sincerely. "But that doesn't mean I haven't missed you and Jake. I've . . . I've just been so busy, that's all."

Yeah, you've been busy, a voice inside his head scoffed. *Busy thinking about how much better your life used to be. You thought having a family would make everything perfect. Boy, were you wrong!*

Tom had originally been ecstatic when George Conroy, his birth father, had entered his life. Although Tom had been dating Elizabeth and had lots of friends, in many ways, since he lost his family, he felt completely alone. Tom couldn't believe his good fortune when Mr. Conroy had showed up in Sweet Valley, along with Jake and Mary. Suddenly Tom had felt as if he had a family again.

But that was before George betrayed me! Tom thought bitterly. Mr. Conroy—his own father—had made a pass at Elizabeth, his perfect, loving girlfriend. Tom hadn't believed her when she had confided in him. In fact, he'd even broken up with her over it, claiming she was jealous of his new family. Tom had been so angry at Elizabeth for what he'd thought were her lies, he'd called her every hideous name in the book and treated her as viciously as possible.

Then Tom found out the awful truth . . . from Mr. Conroy's own mouth, when he admitted to his obsession with Elizabeth. Tom knew that he could never forgive Mr. Conroy for his treachery—or for causing the painful breakup with the only woman he'd ever truly loved. Mr. Conroy and Tom hadn't even spoken since Tom had stormed out of his law office after the confrontation. The only communication they'd had was when Mr. Conroy sent Tom two membership passes to the Verona Springs Country Club.

Big deal! he thought angrily. *So he's got a lot of money. All the money in the world couldn't fill the hole inside me. The only thing that could do that is Elizabeth's love.*

Tom sighed heavily. He closed his eyes briefly, trying to erase the image of Elizabeth. But he couldn't stop thinking about her. *My arms ache to hold her again. If I could just kiss her once more. . . .*

Oh, give it a rest, Watts! he told himself sharply. *Stop acting as if the world has come to an end. You're young, you're healthy, and you've got a beautiful woman who's all over you. What more do you want?*

His thoughts were interrupted as an ice-cream cone was thrust toward his face. "Don't you want some, Tom?" Mary asked, waving the cone back and forth.

41

Tom shook his head slightly to clear his thoughts and had a taste, if only to please his little half sister. The ice cream was delicious, but Tom hardly noticed. *There's only one thing I want.* Tom smiled politely at Dana as she wiped some chocolate chocolate chip ice cream from his face, but he barely knew she was there. *Only one thing, and nothing else matters. I want Elizabeth.*

Denise whistled a tune slightly off-key and swung her purse back and forth as she skipped through the university center. The slight funk that she had been in while shopping with her sorority sisters was gone, and Denise was wearing a smile big enough to match her oversize sunglasses.

"Uh-huh, I'm addicted to love," Denise sang, looking forward to seeing Winston. *It's silly to be unhappy because I don't have a zillion dollars to spend on silk dresses,* she thought. *Why should I be a grump when I've got such a great guy?* "Yeow!"

Denise ricocheted off the edge of a table, sending several brochures fluttering to the ground and a sharp pain through her legs. "Oops! I'm *really* sorry!" Denise spluttered as she bent down to pick up the brochures.

"Let me help." A tall, attractive guy squatted down beside her and began gathering the glossy pamphlets. "Are you OK?"

"Yes, thanks. I guess I wasn't watching where I was going." Denise tried to separate several leaflets that had somehow become stuck together with bubble gum, but the guy took them and tossed them into a nearby wastebasket.

"You mean you weren't coming over to talk to me?" the guy asked with a laugh, returning the brochures to the green felt tabletop as he straightened up.

"No . . . I'm sorry, but do I *know* you?" Denise looked at him more closely. He was definitely cute, with wavy, dark blond hair; but he looked a few years older than most students. Denise sure couldn't place him.

"No, we haven't met. But if you give me a few minutes, I'd like to tell you about my six percent finance rate." His grin crinkled the corners of his eyes.

"Huh?" Denise stared at him in confusion. She rose to her feet, dusting her palms on her dress.

"I'm Andy Newman, with the Only Bank of Gittenbach, New York." Andy's warm brown eyes smiled as he pointed to the name tag on his polo shirt. "We're here at the fair today to offer our card to as many students as possible."

"Fair? What fair? Where is there a fair?" Denise's mind went blank. *Gittenwho? Who is this guy? What is he talking about anyway?*

"The fair is right here." Andy gestured widely.

Denise slowly looked around her. Although she'd been too preoccupied to notice before, she saw now that the center had several brightly colored booths set up. A red banner strung across the university center proudly announced Personal Finance Fair.

"I'd like to tell you about how you get your SVU preapproved gold card today," Andy continued. "You could start enjoying the benefits of our low-interest, risk-free plan immediately."

Gold card? Preapproved? Hello! Denise shook her head, unsure if she'd heard him correctly.

"Interested?" He picked up a clipboard with an application form and gestured to a chair in front of the table.

"You *bet* I'm interested!" Denise sank down in the chair, all thoughts of Winston vanishing from her mind as she gazed up at Andy as if he had sprouted wings and a halo.

"Take a look at the application." Andy tore off one of the application forms and handed it to Denise. "You'll see that our terms are *very* attractive. Only six percent interest, and our minimum monthly payment is quite reasonable."

"I don't get it." Denise's brow furrowed as she pushed her sunglasses back on her head. "Don't I have to have a job?"

"Not at all." Andy shook his head earnestly. "You're a full-time student, so that automatically qualifies you for the SVU gold card. It's true that some credit card companies make employment a stipulation, but not us. The Only Bank wants to be your friend, Denise." Andy smiled sincerely. "We believe in giving students a break. Why wait

44

until you have a job? We know that as a future graduate of this school, your financial prospects are excellent. Here's how it works."

Andy sat down on the corner of the table and handed Denise one of the glossy brochures. The photograph on the front showed a smiling young woman carrying several fancy-looking packages out of an upscale boutique. "We'll start you off with a substantial credit limit so you'll be able to have the benefits of shopping now and paying later." Andy moved closer to Denise and used his pen to point to the center of the application. "Our terms are all spelled out right here. Take a moment to read it over. As you can see, if you go over your limit . . ."

While Andy continued explaining everything patiently, Denise tuned him out. *Terms shmerms!* Denise thought as the words *shop now, pay later* rang in her head. Visions of the peach dress she'd seen at Chris and Candies danced before Denise's eyes. She was much too busy thinking of all the beautiful clothes she could buy to pay much attention to the paragraph that Andy was pointing to. The idea of going out to a fancy restaurant with Winston suddenly seemed much more interesting than listening to Andy Newman from Gittenwhatsit.

". . . So is that clear? Do you have any questions?" Andy finished.

"Huh?" Denise noticed him for the first time in five minutes. "Oh yeah. Questions? Just one. Where do I sign?"

Chapter Three

"Can you believe it, Nick? An A! Professor Phinney gave me an A. He said that even though I missed the exam, he thought my story was *brilliantly* creative. I told you I should go undercover with you!"

Jessica tossed her purple denim jacket over one of the chairs in Nick's living room. They'd just come back from their favorite Mexican restaurant, and Jessica was feeling happy and contented. She hummed a little tune as she flopped down on Nick's leather couch. Kicking off her cowboy boots, she propped up her feet on the glass coffee table between a stack of magazines and a bowl of seashells that they had collected together.

"You thought it would hurt my grades to be so focused on the case, but you were wrong, Nick. It actually *helped* them!"

"OK, so maybe it *was* a good idea for you to go undercover with me," Nick admitted. "But there are other ways to get an A. You could occasionally crack open a few books, Jess." Nick ran a hand through his tousled hair in a way that Jessica found totally irresistible.

"Ha, ha." Jessica grabbed one of the colorful overstuffed pillows that crowded the back of the couch and threw it at Nick. "Say what you like, but Perdita del Mar was an *inspiration*. Not only did she help crack the country club case, but playing her was a lot more fun than sitting through an exam!"

Nick shrugged nonchalantly and began putting Jessica's jacket neatly away.

"Don't you have anything more interesting to do?" Jessica asked as she watched Nick from underneath heavy-lidded eyes. She smiled seductively at him and held out her arms.

He grinned mischievously. "Hmmm . . . now that you mention it, I *did* want to defrost the freezer tonight. . . ."

"Nick Fox! You are the world's most . . . mmm-mm." Jessica's complaint died in her throat as Nick joined her on the couch, sweeping her into his arms. Her insides melted like lava at the touch of his lips, and the feel of his caresses made her want to purr like a kitten.

I always feel so safe when I'm in Nick's arms, Jessica thought as Nick tightened his hold on her. "Mmmm . . . you're the world's best kisser," she murmured against his throat when they finally came up for air.

"Are you sure?" Nick asked anxiously, but his green eyes were sparkling. "I think I might need some more practice." He dipped his mouth to cover Jessica's once more.

Jessica ran her hands over Nick's muscular arms, savoring the rich, spicy scent of his cologne. She sighed with pleasure as Nick nibbled her earlobe.

"Jess, it's been *too* long since we've had a nice, private evening like this. Just the two of us." Nick traced Jessica's delicate profile with his finger.

"I agree completely," Jessica said, shivering at his touch. "Even though I loved going undercover and helping you on a case, I've missed spending quiet time with you."

Nick pulled away and stared at Jessica in amazement. "Quiet time? You've missed spending *quiet* time? I never thought I'd hear Jessica Wakefield say something like that! Quick—a tape recorder!"

Jessica giggled and rapped one of Nick's biceps lightly with her knuckles.

"Listen, if you've missed hanging out, let's make up for it—starting tomorrow," he suggested. "How about we take a picnic to the beach? I'll get some sandwiches from Ruma's and pick you up around ten." Nick brushed several strands of silky blond hair away from Jessica's face.

"That sounds fabulous!" Jessica was practically sparkling with enthusiasm. "My tan needs some serious work."

Jessica loved going to the beach with Nick. Not only was it completely romantic, but he looked totally awesome in a bathing suit. *Those washboard abs, those broad, muscular shoulders . . .* Nick arched an eyebrow and let his gaze linger for a moment on Jessica's long, shapely legs. "Your tan looks pretty good to me," he said huskily.

"You're so sweet, Nick," Jessica cooed. She loved it when Nick spoke to her in that tone of voice. "But seriously, if I want to look my best for the calendar shoot, I really need to be a shade darker."

Nick's brow creased slightly. "Calendar shoot? You mean that Bobby Hornet pinup thing?"

"Of course, Nick." Jessica looked at him, surprised at the sudden change in his tone. "What's wrong?" *He can't be jealous, can he?* she wondered. *We've been through all of this before.*

Nick had been totally supportive of her desire to be in the pinup calendar. But Jessica had left out one little detail—that Bobby Hornet would be involved. Little did she know then that Bobby would end up asking her out! Jessica had been miserable the entire night—and when Nick had caught them together, disaster struck. But everything got smoothed out after Bobby assured Jessica *and* Nick that dating him *wasn't* a job requirement. Still, Jessica couldn't help thinking that Nick was remembering her "date" with Bobby. She couldn't imagine what else could be making him look so sour.

Nick got up from the couch and began to pace restlessly back and forth on the colorful, southwestern-style carpet. "Look, I've had some time to think about it, and . . . I've decided it's not such a good idea." He scowled.

"What . . . is it about posing with Bobby?" Jessica asked delicately. "If you want, I can ask—"

"No." Nick gestured as if he were wiping a table clean with his hands. "It's the whole calendar . . . *thing*. I don't approve."

Jessica's eyes flew wide open in disbelief. "But you said I'd be a natural! You were so encouraging!" Jessica sat upright, dismayed at the expression on Nick's face.

"Well, I've changed my mind, OK? I don't like the idea of a bunch of guys gawking at pictures of my girlfriend—especially when she's *half naked!*" Nick grabbed one of the stools over by the breakfast nook and straddled it.

Jessica's jaw dropped in amazement. "But you were so *proud* when I was picked to be in the calendar!" she cried. "Aren't you proud of me anymore?"

"No!" Nick insisted. "I mean, yes! I mean . . . whatever. It's *not* about that, Jess. It's just—"

"Besides, I'm hardly going to be half naked," she interrupted. "I'll be wearing a bathing suit!"

"Ha!" Nick barked out a laugh. "I've seen some of your bathing suits, Jessica!"

Jessica got up from the couch and stomped over to Nick. "I don't get it, Nick. Why have you changed your mind about this? In case you've forgotten, I *asked* for your opinion before I even *auditioned,* and *you* were *totally* jazzed!"

"I thought you would appreciate the fact that I was trying to protect you, Jessica," Nick explained, his tone softening for a second. "Look, I just don't think that a sleazy calendar is the kind of thing that *my* girlfriend should be involved with." He headed for the refrigerator, grabbed a beer, popped the top, and guzzled it down in one swallow.

"Protect me from what? And just what do you mean by *sleazy?*" Jessica's eyes sparked fire as she wrinkled her nose at Nick's display. "This is going to be a *classy* calendar, Nick! Bobby Hornet wouldn't be involved in anything *sleazy!* It's a tasteful project that's going to raise money for the homeless!"

"Classy? Tasteful?" Nick snorted, crushing the beer can in his fist and tossing it into the trash. "You're even more naive than I thought, Jessica! Do you know the kind of remarks men make about calendar girls? I can assure you they're *not* in very good taste!"

"But Nick, you said that you *wanted* me to pose . . . that you were going to hang a calendar in the station for all your buddies to see!"

"I will *not* have a scantily clad picture of my girlfriend hanging up at every truck stop in the country!" Nick pounded the Formica counter with his fist.

"I thought you were different, Nick," Jessica growled. "You acted so supportive. But you're like every other boyfriend I've ever had! You say you want to *protect* me, but the truth is you're just *jealous* and *possessive!*"

Nick simply stared at her, neither accepting nor denying the charges.

Jessica stalked back and forth furiously. "You said that you didn't want me going on police assignments with you because they were too dangerous. You wanted me to do something nice and safe. Well, I found it! Modeling is about as nice and safe as it gets!"

Of course, Jessica already knew in her heart of hearts that modeling seemed a little *too* nice and safe after the excitement of going on an undercover mission. But even if posing for a calendar was the last thing she wanted to do in the whole world, she wasn't about to give in. Nick didn't deserve that satisfaction right now.

"The truth is that you don't want me to realize *any* of my goals!" she shouted. "You're nothing but a hypocrite, Nick Fox! You just want to crush all my dreams!" Jessica burst into tears and buried her face in her hands. Her slim shoulders heaved as she sobbed.

"Oh, Jess . . . oh, baby." Nick gathered her into his arms and cradled her closely. "I didn't meant to upset you. I'm just being an idiot, that's all." He stroked her back as her sobs began to subside. "I've been so nervous about my own stuff the past few days, I guess I'm just taking out my anxieties on you." He led her gently back to the couch.

"Wh-What are you nervous about?" Jessica sniffed as Nick pulled her onto his lap tenderly.

"The college entrance exams are coming up, and I'm pretty wrecked. I don't know, Jess. I've been hitting the books, but this prelaw stuff seems kind of hard."

What? Entrance exams? she wondered in confusion. *Did I miss something? And doesn't Nick know that he needs to apologize for at* least *ten more minutes?*

"Excuse me . . . I don't think I heard you correctly," Jessica asked as politely as possible. "Did you say . . . college entrance exams?"

"Yeah." Nick nodded. "As of Friday—tomorrow—I'm taking a leave of absence from the force. I think I'm really going to go through with the prelaw thing, Jess."

Jessica pulled her head away from Nick's chest, stunned. After they had finished the country club investigation, Nick had told her that he was considering leaving the force completely and trying prelaw. But he hadn't brought it up since, and she was hoping that he had changed his mind.

"But Nick, if you quit, then we won't be able to work as a team again." Jessica pouted.

"I told you, Jess. We make a great team, but

53

it's just too dangerous. I really want to give school a shot. I don't know if I have a chance, but . . . I'm going to try."

"But *Ni*-ick," Jessica persisted. "You're a *great* cop—the best! That's what you *should* be doing. I mean . . . you're a street-smart kind of guy. You shouldn't be driving yourself crazy studying! School just isn't . . . *you*, you know?"

Nick's face began turning a funny color as Jessica's words hung in the air.

Oops! Jessica worried. *I don't think that came out right. Oh, well, I'm not going to take it back. Nick shouldn't waste his time studying. He is a great cop!*

"*Excuse* me?" Nick sat bolt upright. "What are you saying, that—that I'm just some dumb flatfoot? All brawn and no brain? You don't think I'm smart enough to go to college?" Nick laughed harshly. "Well, I've got news for you. I'm just as smart as anyone else who's applying. Anyway, look who's talking," Nick snarled. "Miss January!"

Gasping in amazement, Jessica jumped up, grabbed her jacket from the closet, and shoved her feet into her boots. "That does it, Nick! You've insulted me once too often tonight. Just remember *I'm* the one who got an A in creative writing!"

"Yeah, and you couldn't have gotten it if I hadn't let you go undercover with me!"

"Chief Wallace let me go undercover with you, in case you don't remember," Jessica cried as she ran

54

to the door. "And by the way, it's Miss *December!*" Tears pouring down her face, she slammed the door so hard, it almost fell off its hinges.

"Let's see . . . there's *Newsweek* . . . *Celebrity Searchlight* . . . *The Sport Report* . . . ," Nina Harper murmured as she plowed through the magazine rack at Le Monde, a chic newsstand and coffee bar just off campus. "C'mon, where is it? It's Monday, right? Doesn't the new issue come out today?"

"It was supposed to," Elizabeth replied. "Maybe it hasn't—"

"Hey, I've got it!" Nina announced happily as she pulled the brand-new issue of *NEWS2US* out from behind the other magazines. She turned to Elizabeth wearing a smile as bright as the sunny yellow dress she had on. "Way to go, girl!" she exclaimed as she and Elizabeth high-fived.

Elizabeth's heart pounded madly. "Let me see!" she demanded, grabbing the magazine from Nina's hands as they walked back to their table.

"So what's the scoop?" Nina asked as they sat down at the green, marble-topped table where cappuccinos and raspberry tarts awaited them. "Come on. Let's read!"

"I'm sort of nervous all of a sudden," Elizabeth admitted with a shy smile.

"You're crazy." Nina laughed, her face shining with warmth. "If I was in an article called 'America's

Hottest Young Physicists,' I'd already have it memorized!"

"You're right. What are we waiting for?" Elizabeth ripped open the magazine and eagerly scanned the table of contents. "Here it is, page . . . twenty-three!" She flipped the pages excitedly to the article, and as she scanned the page dread seeped into her stomach.

Nina gave Elizabeth a concerned look over the rim of her coffee cup. "Is something wrong?"

"I—I don't get it," Elizabeth croaked. She laid the magazine on the table so that Nina could see the photo of her and Scott. Elizabeth blinked to make sure she wasn't dreaming, but when she opened her eyes, she realized with a sinking feeling that she was very much awake.

The picture looked like something out of a true romance magazine. Scott was staring straight at the camera with a confident smile on his face, but Elizabeth only had eyes for him. Her face was tilted upward, and she gazed at him adoringly with sparkling eyes. Elizabeth groaned as she remembered how the photographer had directed her to look up at Scott because there was some kind of shadow on her face. And her eyes! Elizabeth knew that her expression of starry-eyed rapture was the result of having been temporarily blinded from the flash, but to anyone else it would come across as pure devotion.

"It's not that bad," Nina said softly. She put

down her cup and laid a sympathetic hand on Elizabeth's shoulder. "So what if the picture looks a little cheesy? It's the interview that matters."

"Of course," Elizabeth said halfheartedly. "It's just a picture. I'm probably overreacting and . . . ohhh nooo . . ." She trailed off as her eye caught the caption underneath.

Scott Sinclair poses with his girlfriend, the lovely Elizabeth Wakefield, who is following in his spectacular footsteps.

"I can't believe this!" Elizabeth shrieked. "What is this nonsense? His *girlfriend?*" Elizabeth stared at the caption in angry disbelief, but to her dismay, it didn't change. "Where did they get that idea? I can't . . . I just can't *believe* that a woman reporter would write anything so sexist! It's *disgusting!* And what's this *garbage* about following in Scott's footsteps?" she exclaimed furiously. "How *dare* they patronize me like that! I've been writing for *years!*"

Elizabeth took a bite of her raspberry tart to try and calm herself and nearly choked on the delicate pastry. "Here, have mine." She pushed her plate toward Nina. "I can't eat a thing."

"Look, you haven't read the text yet," Nina insisted patiently. "That's going to have a lot of direct quotes from you. It has to get better." She smiled encouragingly.

Elizabeth smiled weakly and nodded. *Maybe Nina's right; maybe it gets better. After all, they* have *to quote what I said about the power of the press.* Gingerly turning the page to the main body of the article, she began reading with a cautious expression as if she were afraid of what she might find. As she skimmed the article she realized she had every reason to be.

They didn't listen to a word I said! I might as well not have even been in the room! Elizabeth thought with raw fury. *Working single-handedly? Am I reading this correctly?* Elizabeth gasped, growing more upset with each word she read. *What about me? What about Nick and Jessica?*

"Uh-oh," Nina began. "I'm getting the feeling that—"

"Nina!" Elizabeth cried. "It gets worse! None of the stuff that I said is in here! I *told* them about Jessica going undercover. . . . Listen to this!"

"I'm not sure I want to."

"'Working single-handedly, brilliant investigative reporter Scott Sinclair was able to solve a case that baffled even the police . . . ,'" Elizabeth read, her voice choking with bitter sarcasm. "This is too much," she said angrily, slamming the magazine on the table. Several of the other patrons turned to stare, but Elizabeth was too upset to notice as she kept reading.

"Liz, it can't be all bad—"

"Well, listen to what it says about me!" She picked up the magazine, struggling to lower her voice. "'Elizabeth Wakefield, who is almost as tal-

58

ented as she is pretty, was able to observe Scott's investigative techniques as she joined him on several fact-finding missions at Verona Springs.'"

"Oh, my—"

"*Almost as talented as I am pretty?* I've heard truck drivers harass women on the street with more respect than that!"

"Well, maybe they misquoted you without meaning to," Nina offered meekly.

"Misquoted me?" Elizabeth snapped. "This goes way beyond misquoting. They didn't *quote* me at *all!* I had such high hopes. . . . This drivel makes it sound as if I was carrying his golf clubs!" Elizabeth thrust the magazine away from her contemptuously. "Or worse, that I'm just his ditzy girlfriend! Oh, Nina! What am I going to do?" Elizabeth buried her face in her hands and groaned.

"I'm really sorry, Elizabeth," Nina said, her forehead creased with concern.

"It's not fair!" Elizabeth whipped up her head, her blue-green eyes dark with anger. "And not just for me either. What about Jessica and Nick? What about Bruce?"

"What about Tom?" Nina filled in.

Elizabeth cringed inwardly as she imagined Tom's reaction to the interview but quickly pushed the agonizing thought aside. "Where did Christine Elliot get this information anyway?" she asked. "What made her think I was Scott's girlfriend? Nothing like this was said while I was in the room. . . ." Elizabeth trailed off as her memory became clearer. Didn't Scott hold her hand in the conference room that day? Right before he said . . .

"I'm going to walk Elizabeth out, but I'll be back in a second if you guys want to hang. . . ."

"Oh no . . . did Scott tell them all this garbage after I left?" she wondered aloud. "No, he wouldn't. . . ."

Wouldn't he? Elizabeth asked herself. In the short time that they'd worked together, Elizabeth had seen that Scott wasn't shy about blowing his own horn—or insisting that he and Elizabeth were dating even when they weren't.

"This has to be Scott's fault," she said quietly.

Nina looked shocked. "Are you sure?"

"No, I'm not sure," Elizabeth admitted. "But I'm going to find out."

"What are you going to do?" Nina whispered.

"I'm going to confront him," Elizabeth said fiercely, stuffing the copy of *NEWS2US* in her backpack. "Sorry, Nina, but I have to go to the *Gazette*. Scott has some pretty fancy explaining to do."

"Hey, do what you gotta do," Nina added supportively as she began gathering up her things.

Jamming her baseball cap on her head, Elizabeth marched out of Le Monde with grim determination.

Tom stared at his office monitor, completely

60

unaware of what he was seeing. He was vaguely conscious of the shapes and images that flickered before him, but for all he knew he was watching footage of hippos in pink tutus.

"So what I thought I'd do here is cut back to a reaction shot instead of panning to the wreckage of the crash," Philip Davis, a new intern, explained earnestly. "What do you think, Tom? Tom?" Philip prompted when Tom failed to respond.

"What? Oh yeah . . . that's a great idea, Philip," Tom said, forcing himself to focus on the screen. He felt bad that he was being so inattentive. Just because *he* was letting thoughts of Elizabeth get in the way of his work didn't mean that he should take it out on his staff. "You really have a creative flair," Tom added sincerely.

Philip's face lit up with the praise as he hit the eject button. "I'll get started on this right away." He waved the videocassette enthusiastically and rushed back to the editing room.

Tom stared at Philip's back with an envious expression. When was the last time he had been that high on work? He couldn't remember. "Sure, you can, pal," Tom said to himself sourly. "The last time you felt that way was when you were working with Elizabeth." Tom grabbed a chewed-up pencil from the chipped mug on his desk and began fiddling with it aimlessly.

Once Tom's office was a place of refuge; now it

just depressed him. Once it had been filled with Elizabeth's laughter and bright energy; now it was empty. Once it had seemed like the den of a hard-boiled reporter; now it just seemed drab. Even the mug on his desk seemed forlorn compared to the bright flowered one that Elizabeth had kept filled with freshly sharpened pencils.

Slamming down the pencil, Tom exhaled raggedly and went over to the old couch with the sprung seat cushions that stood against the wall at the back of the office. *Maybe I just need to lie down,* Tom said to himself as he stretched out. *I didn't get that much sleep last night.* But the couch springs gouged Tom's back uncomfortably.

They never used to bother me, Tom thought. *But then again, I wouldn't have noticed if they were steel spikes because most of the time I spent on this couch was spent kissing Elizabeth.*

Everything in the office seemed to mock him. The reels of footage that ranged the shelves made him think of all the stories they'd covered together. The locked steel cabinet with the camera equipment made Tom think of the first time he and Elizabeth had gone on a shoot. He couldn't even bring himself to look at her abandoned desk. *How can I make things up with her?* Tom asked himself. *What can I do to get her back? I can't go on like this much longer. I just can't.*

As he imagined a future without Elizabeth Wakefield a searing pain ripped through him. Was

62

it only the couch? He knew he would be more comfortable back at his desk, but he didn't move. At least the pain from the springs took his mind off other things. "Yeah, like the pain in my heart," Tom whispered bitterly.

"Tom, can I come in?" Kitty Robertson, another intern, stuck her head around his office door. "I just wanted to drop off the mail."

"Sure, Kitty, come on in." Tom swung himself to his feet and gestured toward his desk. "Just leave it there."

Kitty set the pile down neatly and looked at Tom with concern. "Is everything OK?" she asked gently.

"Yeah, yeah, I'm fine." Tom tried to inject some conviction into his voice, but he knew it was a lost cause. "I'm just really backlogged, that's all." He walked over to his desk and began sorting through the mail.

"Anything I can help with?" Kitty asked solicitously, her hand on the doorknob.

"Nah, thanks for offering. I just need some sleep." Tom smiled at her to show that he appreciated her thoughtfulness.

"Well . . . OK." Kitty nodded and closed the door.

Tom crumpled the junk mail with one hand and tossed it into the wastebasket. He didn't even notice that he had made a perfect three pointer as his eye was caught by the glossy cover of the new issue of *NEWS2US*.

Swallowing hard, he opened the magazine and

slowly turned the pages. He'd heard through the news community grapevine about Elizabeth and Scott's big interview, and even though he had to admit that Elizabeth deserved the coverage, he couldn't help wishing that *he* was the one who had been profiled with her, not that creep Sinclair.

Elizabeth looks beautiful, Tom thought with bittersweet pride as he gazed at her picture. *She really has the most dazzling smile, and her eyes sparkle so brilliantly—but does she have to be staring at Sinclair like that?* Tom grunted in disgust. *She sure never looked at* me *that way!*

But when Tom tore his eyes away from the photo to read the accompanying copy, the caption underneath the picture hit him like a sucker punch to the gut.

"I know Liz is Scott's girlfriend now, but does she have to broadcast it to the world?" Tom's brows knit together in fury as the words sank in. "Following in Scott's footsteps? She's ten times the reporter Sinclair is!"

Tom flipped the page, eager to read how Elizabeth had described his own part in the investigation. "What the . . . 'working single-handedly'? Single-handed, my foot! This article makes Sinclair sound like Edward R. Murrow! 'Brilliant investigative reporter.'" Tom snorted. "In his dreams, maybe!" He turned the pages fruitlessly, looking for continued coverage that would mention his efforts along with those of Jessica, Nick, and Bruce. But the article didn't even acknowledge them—and what he *did* find horrified him even more.

"'Scott and Elizabeth are just as hot a couple off the record as they are on,'" he read aloud, incredulousness rising in his voice. "Breaking the Verona Springs story was hard work, but the two still found plenty of time to unwind in each other's arms after a tough day on the job.'" Tom blinked, unable to comprehend the words. *"What?"*

With an agonized groan Tom crushed the magazine furiously in his hands and threw it in the trash along with the junk mail. "There's no way Elizabeth could have had anything to do with this garbage," he muttered angrily. "This isn't her fault—it's Sinclair's!"

Tom paced around his office briskly. "There's something wrong here," he said, his mind racing. "How can I . . . I've got it!" Tom snapped his fingers and rummaged in the desk drawer for his address book. "M—Mallon, Marshall, Martins!" He snatched up his phone and dialed Dave Martins, a casual friend of his who had interned over at *NEWS2US*. He and Tom had met several times at journalism seminars. Tom respected him as a reporter, and was sure that he could count on him for help.

He tapped his foot nervously, mentally preparing what he would say to Dave. "All I know is, something isn't right," Tom fumed. "Elizabeth got slammed—and Sinclair is so low, he must be at the bottom of it."

Chapter Four

There's Scott—trapped like the rat he is, Elizabeth thought as she stomped into the *Gazette* offices and dumped her backpack on the desk they shared with a force that made him jump. Several of Scott's cherished mementos, including a signed photograph of Joseph Pulitzer, went crashing to the floor. Ordinarily Elizabeth would have been horrified to wreak such destruction, but right now the sound of the glass shattering only soothed her.

Of course Scott would still be here while everyone else is out to lunch, Elizabeth thought with a vicious, silent snicker. *Where else would such a dedicated newshound be?* Still, she was glad the offices were empty. Elizabeth intended to tell Scott off in no uncertain terms, and the privacy meant she could yell louder.

"Hey, Liz, is something wrong?" Scott's gaze slid

away from Elizabeth's furious face to the backpack on the desk, where the copy of *NEWS2US* had fallen out. Judging by the way Scott stiffened, Elizabeth knew he must have read the article. He swallowed hard and avoided Elizabeth's eyes.

At least he has the grace to be embarrassed, Elizabeth thought. *Well, hold on to your hat because you have no idea how bad you're about to feel!*

Leaning forward, she placed her hands firmly on the desk. "Why don't *you* tell *me* what's wrong, Scott? You're such a *brilliant* investigative reporter—I'm sure you'll have no trouble figuring it out!" Elizabeth's eyes bored into Scott's with an intensity that made him flinch.

"Elizabeth, I was as upset as you were when I read the article," Scott said softly. For once his confident exterior seemed shaken. "Truly, I was stunned. Why do you think I didn't call you?" Scott ran a hand through his hair nervously. "You know, I woke up first thing this morning and rushed to get a copy as soon I could. I'd even picked up some fresh croissants because I'd hoped we could read the article together over breakfast." He shook his head and winced. "I was so excited about the article—until I read it. I didn't know what to do or where to turn. I wanted to talk to you about it, but I was too embarrassed and insulted—for you."

Elizabeth gave Scott a hard stare. He sounded sincere, and he certainly looked more distraught than she'd ever seen him. She felt herself softening a bit, but she still had too many unanswered questions. "Where did the reporter get this information from, then?" Elizabeth demanded, her voice steely.

Scott leaned back in his chair and laced his fingers behind his head. A shadow of his former cockiness appeared as he gave Elizabeth a small smile. "You know, if it wasn't such a ridiculous cliché, I'd have to say that you look beautiful when you're angry."

Elizabeth's mouth dropped open in shock at the blatant sexism of the remark. "That has to be one of the most offensive compliments I've ever gotten," Elizabeth sputtered in disbelief. "Besides the fact that it was completely patronizing, it has absolutely *nothing* to do with what we're discussing."

"But don't you see, Elizabeth? It has *everything* to do with the topic under discussion." Scott leaned forward, his voice soft. "Don't you ever look in the mirror? Don't you know the effect you have on other women? Do you have any idea just how *threatening* you really are?"

"If you're trying to cover up something, it's not working!" Elizabeth fumed. "Save the two-bit compliments for some high-school intern."

"Listen, Elizabeth." Scott colored slightly. "I didn't mean to be offensive or inappropriate, but I *did* mean to shock you. To make you look at things with a little perspective. You really don't know what I'm talking about, do you?"

Elizabeth shook her head silently. *Let's see how Scott talks his way out of this one!* she thought angrily.

"Look—put yourself in Christine Elliot's shoes for a second." Scott got up from his chair and began pacing back and forth. "Imagine you're a second-string reporter, and you've been given a fluff assignment. I mean, let's face it—getting profiled in *NEWS2US* may be a big deal for you and me, but from Christine Elliot's point of view she's just a hack who's stuck covering campus news."

"So?" Elizabeth began slowly. "What does that have to do with—"

"It has *everything* to do with it," Scott interrupted. "Christine Elliot, who's not *that* accomplished, comes out here on what she assumes is a puff piece, and what does she find?" Scott paused dramatically and waved his hand toward Elizabeth like a magician unveiling his master trick. "She finds Elizabeth Wakefield. Ten years younger, ten times more accomplished, and ten times more beautiful. How do you think that made her feel?"

"Well, what made her think that you were working alone? And where did she get the idea that I was your girlfriend? C'mon, Scott, can you *honestly* tell me that you didn't have any part in the way the article came out?"

"Elizabeth, you have to know that even if I wanted to, I don't have any control over what some other reporter writes." Scott paused for a second. "Look. After you left, Christine asked a ton of questions about you. She wanted to see your clips, and I could tell she was blown away by how good a writer you are." Scott placed his hands on Elizabeth's shoulders and looked deeply into her eyes. "She said that since you weren't available to go for that coffee, maybe she could take your place."

Elizabeth squinted. "I don't catch your drift."

"She *totally* came on to me, Elizabeth."

"What?"

"I'm serious." Scott tightened his hold on Elizabeth's shoulders. "Of course I said no, but that was a mistake—a *big* mistake. She immediately got *very* offended. I just figured there was nothing I could do at that point and that it didn't really matter." Scott shook his head. "Was I wrong. I see it all now. She was so jealous of you, Elizabeth, and my rejecting her was like the straw that broke the camel's back. I guess she just decided to get at you the only way she could. She totally shafted you. She knew what a brilliant reporter you are, but I'm sure it made her feel great to make you look like an idiot. That stuff about you being my girlfriend was just her way of making you seem as incompetent as possible."

"That can't be true," Elizabeth whispered.

"I'm not a creative enough writer to make up something like this."

"It's just so hard to believe," she murmured.

"I know it is, Liz," Scott replied as he began picking up his scattered possessions from the floor. "Someone with your kind of journalistic integrity could never imagine stooping so low. But not everyone is like you."

Elizabeth sat on the edge of the desk, stunned. She wanted to believe him. It was far more comforting—in a weird way—that this was all some kind of back-stabbing ploy by a threatened reporter than a betrayal by one who—for once—seemed to actually care about her.

Could it really be true? Elizabeth thought. She wasn't conceited, but she would have to be made of stone to resist the idea that Christine Elliot was jealous enough of both her talent *and* her looks to slam her that way.

Unlike most women, Elizabeth was truly able to see her physical self objectively. All she had to do was look at her twin sister, Jessica. She saw the kinds of reactions Jessica got from both men *and* women. *Why is it so hard for me to believe that people could respond to me the same way?* Elizabeth wondered. *And—OK—I know I'm good at what I do. Is it so far-fetched that a professional reporter for a respected newsmagazine would envy my talent too?*

Elizabeth's anger began to back away. *Maybe I'm the jealous one here. Maybe I'm just envious that Scott got such great coverage. Who knows? Even if*

71

Scott hadn't resisted Christine's advances, I still might have come off badly.

Reluctantly Elizabeth remembered how flustered she had been during the interview, how she'd let herself be thrown off by the uncomfortable seating and the photographer's flash. The whole thing seemed probable. In fact, it was most likely completely true. Why would Scott lie to her about something so serious?

"OK, Scott," she began with a nod. "If you say that's what happened, then I believe you." As she looked away for a second her gaze fell on the smashed photograph. Shame coursed through her like a virus. "Oh no—your picture! I'm so sorry. . . . I shouldn't have burst in here like that. It was childish."

Scott waved his hand at her apology. "The last thing you have to do is apologize. Believe me—if I thought that you were responsible for bad-mouthing me to the press, I'd be plenty mad too."

Elizabeth smiled. "Thanks for being straight with me." She crouched down and picked up Scott's few remaining belongings from the floor. "I'm going to be getting back to Dickenson now— you look pretty busy. I'll see you tomorrow."

"Wait, Liz, I . . ." Scott trailed off and shook his head. "Never mind. I'll see you tomorrow."

Elizabeth paused as she picked up her backpack. "What?"

"Well, this may not be the most appropriate

time to bring it up, but I've had some good news, and I wanted to share it with you."

"Oh, come on! Just because I got a little bent out of shape over the article doesn't mean that you can't tell me the good news. Besides, I'm over the *NEWS2US* thing now." She hoped Scott accepted her lie. She still was hurting, but her embarrassment over trashing Scott's side of the desk was too strong for her to let on.

"I was accepted," Scott said simply.

It took Elizabeth a moment to realize what he was talking about. "Accepted? To DCIR? Scott, that's fabulous!"

"Thanks." Scott shrugged nonchalantly.

Elizabeth tried to match Scott's casual attitude, but she couldn't help doubting that her application would be as successful. She *was* sincerely happy for Scott. But the humiliation and anger that she'd felt earlier came rushing back as if they'd never left.

Her face began to burn as words from the article flashed before her eyes. Maybe Scott hadn't betrayed her in the way she thought he had, but what did that matter? The end result was still the same. The interview had made her look like a totally incompetent journalist who was only in the game because she was holding on to someone's coattails. There was no way that any admissions committee reading that article would want to have anything to do with her.

Let's face it, Elizabeth told herself bitterly. *That article made it seem as if the only thing I ever do with a newspaper is read the comics. My chances of getting into DCIR are history!*

"You sure make my job easy, sugar," cooed Andre, Jessica's calendar-shoot makeup artist, as he stood back to survey his handiwork. Cocking his head to one side, Andre mixed several lip gloss colors together on a palette before tinting Jessica's lips a sultry red.

Easy? Jessica stared at him in disbelief. "I'd hate to know what *hard* is," she spluttered as Andre finished with her mouth and moved on to her lashes.

Already Jessica had spent four hours in the makeup chair. She'd come in with freshly washed hair and what was, at least in *her* opinion, full makeup that could turn any supermodel green with envy. She'd been surprised when Andre had taken it all off instantly—and even more surprised when he insisted on rewashing her hair with a special volumizing shampoo.

But the biggest shock of all came with the body makeup. Even though Jessica was tanned an even, golden honey, four of Andre's assistants had taken *two hours* to paint on the eight different colors of base that constituted the perfect shade of tan that Bobby Hornet favored.

At least they didn't have to redo all their hard

work, Jessica thought grimly. Richard, the photographer on the shoot, had reduced one of the other girls to tears when he insisted that her skin was too pasty. *Her* body makeup had taken *three* hours to redo!

"Believe me, sugar, you don't *know* what hard is," Andre drawled. "Some of the top models require days of camouflage. Why, some of them even have *freckles!*" Andre shuddered with horror. He continued to regale Jessica with tales from the fashion world, but for once she wasn't interested.

Now I understand why Elizabeth keeps insisting that the media promotes unrealistic images of women, she thought in amazement. *I mean, four hours for makeup, and I'm not even* done *yet? And most of the other models are getting even more work than I am!* Jessica glanced at the other models, each in her own chair, each with her own makeup artist. *We look as if we're cars on an assembly line.*

"How much longer will this take?" Jessica whined.

"Shouldn't be long now, hon. Maybe another hour and a half. Of course, Richard and Bobby have the final say."

"Grrreat," Jessica said with barely concealed sarcasm. She covered her mouth as she yawned.

Andre's jaw dropped in apparent alarm. "Don't mess with your mouth, sugar! I've just *finished* that."

Jessica rolled her eyes in extreme boredom.

What made me think I ever wanted to be a model? she wondered. At first she had reveled in the attention that the crew had showered on her. *But after three hours of lighting technicians staring at me—no, practically* drooling—*I've had enough attention to last me for a lifeti . . . well, enough attention to last me for days anyway!* Jessica gave a sudden start as Tony, one of the too-attentive lighting technicians, appeared at her elbow.

"Can I get you a drink, Ms. Wakefield? Some sparkling water?"

"That would be nice," Jessica began, nearly jumping out of her skin at Andre's shriek.

"Are you trying to drive me to an early grave?" Andre cried. "I just finished the lower half of her face!"

"Is something wrong?" Bobby Hornet came over to see what had caused Andre's outburst.

"Just dying of boredom," Jessica murmured. Months earlier she would have passed out from excitement at the mere *idea* that *the* Bobby Hornet would someday approach her and speak in her presence. But between the disastrous dinner she'd had with him and her now total disinterest in the upcoming shoot, she had no excitement left to share.

Bobby sat down beside her, his eyes sparkling as he took her hand. When he casually tossed his hair over one shoulder, Jessica concealed a smile.

She'd always thought that his long, tousled dark mane was sexy, but now it just looked silly to her. She had watched in stunned silence as three stylists sprayed and coifed him and—as the finishing touch—discreetly added hair extensions to give his hair an exaggerated fullness.

"We certainly wouldn't want one of the most beautiful models on the shoot to die, would we?" Bobby teased, increasing the pressure on her hand.

Jessica resisted the urge to roll her eyes again. She certainly wasn't worried about Bobby hitting on her—he knew now that she was dating Nick Fox, who served in the same precinct as Bobby's brother. Still, his attention was getting cloying. He'd come over to check on her at least every fifteen minutes.

Did Nick put him up to this? she wondered. *Well, if Nick thinks that securing Bobby's personal attention on me and me only would be helpful somehow, he's sadly mistaken!* The only thing it had done was make the other models jealous.

"Something wrong, angel?" Bobby asked, his face concerned.

"I just need a *break*, Bobby," Jessica complained. "My legs are falling asleep from sitting still for so long."

"Good idea." Bobby stood up and clapped. "Listen up, everybody. We're on break—fifteen minutes. Johnny," Bobby called to one of his assistants, "pump up the volume!"

As the soft, driving rhythm of Bobby Hornet's signature sound filled the air, Jessica slid down from her chair gratefully and went to the refreshment table. A few other models followed her, but most of them whipped out hand mirrors and began scrutinizing their faces.

"Girls, girls, remember to use straws!" Andre shrilled over the music. "We can redo color intensity, but we simply *can't* redraw lip lines. And don't have anything more fattening than mineral water." He snatched a glass of bubbly water from one model's hand. "*Non*sparkling. Carbonation bloats!"

"I had no idea modeling was such a drag," Jessica remarked to Tammy Verdi, a stunning redhead from Delta Tao.

"Really?" Tammy raised her perfectly arched eyebrows in surprise. "I would have thought that you had a lot of modeling experience."

Jessica downed her water with a small shrug. "Thanks . . . I guess." Once she would have been thrilled to have someone think she was a model. But now she couldn't imagine who would possibly want to be one—ever. The only interest anyone had in her was whether the lights caught the artificial hollows that Andre had painted under her cheekbones or played up the pouty mouth that glistened seductively.

Suddenly she felt as if she were being peeled like a banana. With a start, she realized that a different lighting technician was staring at her. Shivering slightly, she crossed her arms in front of her chest. *Nick was right—I am half naked!* Jessica thought miserably.

"You know, *I've* done quite a bit of modeling," Linda Freeman, a sophisticated brunette from Delta Epsilon Delta, joined in.

"Really? How *fascinating*," Jessica said politely, suppressing a yawn. She couldn't bear sitting through another marathon makeup session ever again. She wondered how Linda managed.

"So have I," Tiffany Thomas from Omega house simpered. "Of course, I've mostly worked in Europe."

"Well, I've never worked in Europe, but I *have* done several swimwear shoots." Alissa Monder, a sophisticated ash blonde from Delta Phi, turned to Jessica with a smile. "And I have to say, I would *kill* to have your body."

"Really?" Jessica asked, flattered, as she took in Alissa's flawless figure. She didn't exactly appreciate being ogled by lighting technicians, but Jessica could always handle a sincere compliment. "I don't see why, but thanks."

"Oh, I know I look good enough to model." Alissa flipped back her silvery mane. "But I always need extra body makeup. You see, I'm an outie."

"An outie?" Jessica's brow wrinkled in confusion as the other models nodded in apparent sympathy.

"You know, an *outie*," Alissa said. "My belly button sticks out. You, on the other hand, are a perfect innie."

"I'm a perfect innie?" Jessica repeated, stunned. *Is she crazy?* she wondered. *I mean, how shallow can you get? A perfect belly button? That's the stupidest thing I've ever heard!*

Bobby Hornet sauntered over. "So, what do you think of my new single, Jessica?"

Grateful for the distraction, Jessica nodded along with the melody floating out from the speakers. "I like it," she said enthusiastically. "It has a great beat for dancing." *At least Bobby is creative,* she reasoned. *Making music is so much more impressive than modeling. Belly buttons don't matter much on the top ten, do they?*

"I wanted to know your take on it." Bobby smiled. "It's really important, you know?"

"Well, you know me," Jessica said earnestly. "I *live* for what's important and ignore the rest."

"OK—so which picture do you think I should use for the cover?" Bobby asked hastily, passing Jessica a set of contact sheets. "I'm leaning toward the shot in the leather vest, but I don't know. My chest hair looks a little too unruly. Maybe the retoucher—"

Jessica slammed the prints down in frustration. "What is *wrong* with you people? Don't you have anything *important* to think about?"

Not surprisingly, Jessica's outburst was greeted

with stunned silence—even *she* was a little rattled by her Elizabethan accusation. She stared at everyone defiantly, her hands on her hips.

"Excuse me, Jessica," Tammy piped up, a snide expression on her face. "But just who do you think you are? A physics professor or something? I'm sure if I looked at your checkbook, I'd see that you spend as much money on beauty products as the rest of us."

Jessica flushed. "Maybe that *used* to be true, but these days I have a lot more *important* things on my mind. You guys probably wouldn't know this, but I just helped the police solve a murder." She glowed with pride. "So, OK, Tammy. Maybe it wasn't rocket science, but it came pretty close!"

The blank looks around Jessica fueled her rage. "Golly! Don't you people ever read the papers or watch the news? The Verona Springs scandal was *everywhere!*"

"Oh, I get it." Bobby clapped his hand on Jessica's shoulder and laughed patronizingly. "Jessica's boyfriend, Nick, is a cop, everyone. He must have been telling you about the details of a case or something."

"Not at all!" Jessica stamped her foot. "Well, Nick *was* working on the case, but so was I! I was his partner!"

"Sure, Jess." Bobby nodded. "Was Sherlock Holmes part of the team too? Perry Mason? Matlock?"

"Oh, that's *rich*, Bobby," Jessica drawled in a tone icy enough to let everyone know it was anything but. "Here're some words of advice—keep your day job."

As she turned away from Bobby she noticed Andre sitting in the corner, reading the new issue of *NEWS2US*. "Ha!" she cried, pouncing on Andre and snatching the magazine away. "So you don't believe I helped bring down a murderer, huh? Well, read this and weep!"

Jessica excitedly flipped through the magazine, found the article, and tossed it over to Bobby. "Feast your eyes and apologize."

"So your sister is dating a reporter. Big deal." Bobby shrugged and tossed the magazine back to Jessica.

Huh? Jessica scanned the article. *OK, maybe it does say that, but what does it say about the investigation?* Jessica searched eagerly through the body of the text for information about her role in the case—a mention of her name—anything.

"Verona Springs is an exclusive club. . . ." Blah blah blah . . . *"Paul Krandall . . ."* C'mon, where's all the stuff about me? . . . *"Working single-handedly, brilliant investigative reporter Scott Sinclair"* . . . ?

"Single-handedly?" Jessica breathed. She closed the magazine, too stunned to continue reading. *OK, that was just my imagination,* Jessica told herself. *All these hot lights have affected my vision. I'll just close my eyes for a second. . . .*

Jessica counted to ten, opened her eyes, and reopened the magazine. *I just don't believe it!* she thought, enraged, as she realized there wasn't a single mention of her in the article. *I worked so hard! Elizabeth wouldn't do this to me, would she?*

"Bobby!" Richard, the photographer, called impatiently. "I'm ready to get started over here. We've been set up for the last ten minutes. We're wasting time, so let's move it!"

"We're ready," Bobby announced, and all the models ran over to Richard excitedly.

But Jessica stood rooted to the spot, oblivious to everything else. She read the text of the article once more, her heart sinking with every word. Hot tears pricked beneath her eyes. How could her hard work go unappreciated? And how could she be humiliated in front of all these brainless robots?

"What's your problem, Jessica?" Bobby quirked an eyebrow. "So your joke didn't play. Who cares? You're still going to be a sensation in the swimsuit calendar. That's what really matters."

No, it isn't, Jessica said to herself. *I want something more. I don't know what yet, but being in a calendar and being treated like a bimbo certainly* isn't *what matters!*

"If you're done with your little scene, we can all get going," Richard hollered peevishly. "We don't have all day."

Jessica squared her shoulders in determination. *I won't show them how miserable I am,* she told herself. *I'm not going to give them the satisfaction!* She approached Bobby, who stood in front of a backdrop painted the flaming colors of a California sunset. She was surprised at first to be posing in front of a cardboard backdrop when all the glories of a real California sky were waiting just outside the door, but soon enough that made total sense. Modeling was cheap. Cheap and phony.

"Jessica!" Richard lowered his camera. "Do you think you could put a *little* effort into this? After all, this is the *cover shot,* and Bobby chose you for it. Don't make us second-guess his taste, OK?"

Jessica forced a smile, but inside she was a tangled mass of emotions. *I just want to get this whole thing over with,* she thought, hot tears of humiliation burning behind her eyes. *I'm tired of being appreciated only for my looks. From now on I want* respect!

Chapter
Five

"Juliet's balcony is ninety degrees to the ground and sixteen feet high," Nick Fox read aloud. "Romeo uses a twenty-foot ladder, which reaches the balcony. What is the angle of incline of the ladder?"

Angle of incline? Who cares? Besides, it sounds as if Romeo is in for a broken neck! Nick thought wryly.

Nick closed the heavy blue trigonometry book with a sigh and pushed it away from him. He had been preparing for the college entrance exams diligently, but as far as he was concerned, he knew less now than before he'd started studying. He rubbed his hands over his face, trying to scrub away the heavy feeling of fatigue. "I'm a little tired right now, that's all," Nick consoled himself. "Maybe I'll tackle something easier. Save math until I've covered the vocab."

He reached out his hand for another book. With a shock Nick realized that the formerly huge pile on his left side only had one volume left. The rest had been pushed over to his right, to be "tackled later" along with trig.

Nick groaned miserably. "Come on, *all* these books can't be too hard for me!" He drew the last one toward him: *How to Build an Erudite Vocabulary: Your Guide to Conquering the SATs.* "I don't even understand the title!" Nick complained, pushing the unopened book away from him.

"Who am I kidding? When was the last time I read anything other than a case file anyway?" Nick got up from the dining-room table and went into the kitchen, wincing at the mess that greeted him there. Countless coffee cups lay overturned, dozens of crushed beer cans were overflowing from the wastebasket, a puddle of spilled tomato soup made a bright red splotch on the white counter, and the sink overflowed with dishes. Nick was normally a spotless housekeeper, but he'd been too busy being a cop *and* studying for the college entrance exams to keep things clean. "The place looks as if Jess was crashing here for a few days," Nick muttered, grabbing a paper towel and going to work on the counter.

Jessica. Nick paused as an image of her face flashed before him. *I wish our last date hadn't ended so badly,* he thought, his heart contracting painfully as he remembered the evening. They

86

hadn't spoken since then, and he missed her terribly. He stared at the phone uncertainly. Should he call her?

And tell her what—that she was right? Nick asked himself sarcastically. The past few days he had been too busy to dwell on what she'd said, but now her words hit him full force.

Street-smart.

Well, if the time he'd spent studying had showed him anything, it was that he sure wasn't book-smart. Nick put down the paper towel and walked over to the mirror hanging in the living room. The frame was jam-packed with pictures of him and Jessica, but he didn't notice them as he looked at himself head-on.

Who am I? he asked himself.

He was a cop.

"Who am I *kidding?*" Nick laughed. He was a guy who should be walking the beat, not walking into a courtroom carrying a fancy leather briefcase and wearing a silk tie. With his rugged face and broken nose, Nick had to admit that he didn't look like any lawyer he'd ever seen. He rolled his T-shirt sleeve up past the pumped-up biceps Jessica loved and stared at the tattoo on his shoulder.

What kind of lawyer has a tattoo? Nick asked himself. *I bet the closest most defense attorneys have been to a tattoo is when they visit their clients in prison.* Nick stared dolefully at the three intertwined roses before yanking down the sleeve.

He walked away from the mirror, his feet shuffling along in the scuffed leather slippers he liked to wear at home. Jessica always made fun of them, but Nick had explained to her that years of walking the streets before he'd made detective had given him flat feet. The slippers were the only comfortable shoes he owned, but still he kicked them off in disgust. Comfortable or not, they just reminded him that he had flat feet. As far as Nick was concerned, they were just one more sign that he wasn't cut out to be a lawyer.

Nick's eyes roamed the room. He paused to look at the trophy he'd received as rookie of the year. His framed graduation certificate from the police academy hung above it. Would a law-school diploma ever hang beside it?

Not if you don't get back to studying, he told himself with a sigh. He trudged back into the dining room, but just looking at the pile of books made him tired.

"Wake up and smell the coffee," Nick muttered. "You're just not cut out for this academic stuff. Why not stick with what you're really good at?"

With determination Nick grabbed his motorcycle jacket from the back of a chair and found his work boots under a pile of dirty laundry. He'd had enough of hitting the books. It was time to hit the streets.

Anxiously Tom lunged for the phone before it even had time to ring twice, praying that it was

Dave Martins calling with the information on *NEWS2US* he'd promised. "Hello?"

"Hey, Tom, it's Dave."

"Dave! What've you got for me, buddy?"

"Listen, I found out some pretty interesting stuff."

Tom tried to act casual, but his heart rate sped up instantly. "What did you find?" *I hope it's good,* he added silently. He grabbed a yellow legal pad from his desk, and cradling the phone against one ear, he rummaged in the top drawer of his desk for a pen.

"OK—I didn't want to ask anyone outright about this Sinclair guy," Dave began. "I thought it would seem too obvious. So I went to Kate Langford, the features editor, with a copy of the magazine. I told her the young journalists profile was really great and asked if it would be a continuing feature."

"And?"

"I said that if it was, I'd be really jazzed about being the next one interviewed." Dave laughed. "I really buttered her up: 'Since I know you're so influential here at *NEWS2US,* is there any way you could help me swing that?' You know, I just kept going with it. 'What's the selection process? Who's this Sinclair guy anyway?'"

"Brilliant," Tom said, impressed.

"Well, that's when things started to heat up. Kate said that she wasn't sure who this Wakefield girl was, but she sure had a pretty good idea of how Sinclair was chosen."

Tom gripped the phone excitedly. "And?"

"And . . . check this out. *NEWS2US* is one of the companies owned by Morgan Media Holdings. Morgan Media Holdings is a *very* powerful media conglomerate. They own the *Tribune,* the—"

"I know, I know," Tom cut him off impatiently. Of course he knew about Morgan Media. How could he be in the news business and not know? They were one of the most powerful media groups in the world. But what did that have to do with Slimebucket Sinclair?

"Well, did you know who has one of the most powerful positions on the board?"

"Cut to the chase, Martins," Tom barked, unable to stand the suspense any longer.

"There are three big wheels over at Morgan, but the biggest is a fellow by the name of James Sinclair."

"A relative?" Tom asked, his hand racing across the legal pad as he frantically took notes.

"His *father.*"

Tom let out a low whistle. "Connections can't get more high-level than that, can they?" His stomach churned with excitement and shock at the news. "No wonder the guy got such gushy press! Sounds a little unethical to me, don't you think?"

"Yeah. But to be fair, Kate *did* say that she wasn't a *hundred* percent sure if that's why Scott was chosen. I'd hate to convict someone on hearsay."

"Yeah, yeah, so would I. But the connection seems pretty strong to me."

"Wait up, buddy. You haven't let me get to the best part."

"There's more?" Tom asked eagerly.

"There's more," Dave confirmed. "Kate said that for all she knew, this guy *was* a brilliant journalist who fully deserved to be profiled, connections or no connections."

Tom snorted derisively. "Yeah, right."

Dave laughed. "Just what has this guy done to you, buddy?"

You don't want to know, Tom replied silently. "Go on."

"OK. So Kate said that Sinclair must have quite a bit of talent because she'd just heard through the grapevine that he was accepted to this really first-class journalism school. You know, the one in Denver."

"The Denver Center for Investigative Reporting?"

"Yeah, that's the one."

I hope he takes it, Tom thought, his heart fluttering at the prospect. *Then he'd be far away from Liz.*

"I couldn't believe it," Dave insisted. "I mean, their programs are way beyond awesome. They only look at the top students in the country. We're talking triple-A, top-of-the-dean's-list, solid-gold students. Probably ninety percent of the Pulitzer Prize winners in the last ten years have been alumni. To tell you the truth, Tom, when I heard that, I figured he *did* deserve that article."

Tom's heart sank as he listened. This was exactly the kind of information he *didn't* want to hear. "Great. Is *that* what you called to tell me?" Tom asked sarcastically, pounding his desk in frustration. "That Scott Sinclair really *is* an ace reporter? Thanks for nothing."

"Listen, Watts, I didn't know *what* to think. I checked out the Internet to see what more I could come up with. You know, any PR about DCIR. Maybe they had a charter that said they had to take one charity case a year, and Sinclair was it."

"Let me guess—Scott got in on the sympathy vote. They decided to take the guy whose personal essay made him sound like the biggest sleaze."

Dave laughed. "Well, not exactly. Anyway, I got the usual stuff about what a terrific program it is, rah-rah-rah and all that. I was just about to give up the whole thing when I saw a red flag."

Tom gripped the receiver so hard that his knuckles turned white. "Let me have it."

"The undergraduate program that Scott got into is totally underwritten by *Morgan Media Holdings!* I don't know about you, but from where *I* stand, that's one coincidence too many."

"Yes!" Tom raised his fist in a victory punch. "I seriously owe you, Dave."

"Hey, I was glad to help. You can buy me a beer sometime."

"Would you settle for a bottle of champagne?"

Dave chuckled. "I think I can handle that."

"I mean it, Dave. You really came through for me. Call me anytime if I can return the favor."

"Maybe you can nominate me to be profiled in the next *NEWS2US*."

"Hey, you deserve it. I'll catch you later."

"Later."

Tom hung up the phone and began flipping through the office schedule. In order to get the piece forming in his mind on that evening's newscast, he needed to assemble a camera crew as of five minutes ago.

Wait until Elizabeth hears what I have to say, Tom thought, scribbling down his key ideas for the report. *Once she hears how Scott used his father's power to further his own ambitions, she won't want to touch him with a ten-foot pole!*

I really needed to get out of my apartment, Nick thought with a satisfied smile. He'd been walking for hours, and the fresh air had pumped new life into him. He'd had some time to reevaluate his priorities too. Being a cop had plenty of good things to recommend it. Could he really just give it up like that?

"After all," he murmured, "I wouldn't have met Jessica if I hadn't been on an undercover assignment."

Nick would never forget the first time he'd seen her. He'd been hanging out at the SVU student center, trying to meet people, and then . . . *bam!* There was the most beautiful woman he'd ever seen. He'd only approached her because she'd seemed popular and well connected enough to know who might be part of the dangerous SVU drug ring he'd been investigating. Little did he know that Jessica Wakefield would become the love of his life.

Meeting Jessica is the best fringe benefit a cop ever had, Nick thought. Although she drove him crazy at times, he'd never loved a woman more. But loving Jessica had its problems too.

"In fact, if it wasn't for her, I probably wouldn't have thought of leaving the force in the first place," Nick mumbled, frowning. He knew that Jessica's appetite for excitement had only been whetted by her assisting him at Verona Springs. If he stayed on the force, there would be no stopping her; she'd insist on accompanying him as often as possible. But what if she got hurt? Injured? Even killed? Nick swallowed hard at the thought. He knew that if anything happened to Jessica because of him, he would never be able to forgive himself.

Quickly Nick's upbeat mood evaporated. "What am I so worried about?" he asked himself. "I'm going to quit and start college just so something like that *can't* happen." But did he really have a chance at getting into college? Judging from his studying abilities, he was well on his way to failing the entrance exams.

Get a grip, he told himself harshly. His stomach rumbled in response, and Nick realized that his last meal had been the half can of tomato soup that *hadn't* spilled on the counter. Spying a diner across the street, he made a beeline for it.

Nick made his way over to a booth in the corner and settled in against the cracked red vinyl seat. He studied the laminated menu and quickly made a selection. "Corned beef and Swiss on rye, fries, extra-hot mustard, extra-large cola," he told the waitress.

As he waited for his order Nick drummed his fingers on the Formica tabletop, feeling slightly bored. Going to restaurants by himself wasn't his favorite thing to do. So when he spied a discarded magazine left on one of the other tables, he went over to pick it up.

"Oh yeah, *NEWS2US*," he murmured. "I wonder if Elizabeth is in this issue?" His sandwich was waiting for him on his own table when he returned. He picked it up, took a healthy bite, and flipped to the interview.

Wow—Elizabeth is pretty crazy about Scott, he realized when he saw the accompanying photograph. *I didn't think they were that hot and heavy.* From what he'd seen of Scott during the country club investigation, he didn't seem like the kind of guy Elizabeth would go for. Still, there was no denying Scott had a certain smooth charm, and Nick knew some women really went for that.

Nick took a long drink of his soda as he turned the page. His brow creased in confusion as he read the text. *I don't get it,* he told himself. *Didn't anyone mention . . . wait a minute.* "Working single-handedly"? *Scott?* He choked on an inhaled french fry so loudly that several other patrons turned to stare. *What is this, science fiction? I thought this was supposed to be a hard-hitting* newsmagazine!

"I don't believe it," he muttered angrily as he finished reading the exaggerated copy. "This article makes Scott come across like some kind of hero! It sounds as if all he had to do was jump into a phone booth, put on his cape, break a date with Lois Lane, and crack the case!" Nick bit into his sandwich viciously and considered giving Chief Wallace a call. He'd probably want to hire this one-man homicide-and-robbery division.

Then again, why would Scott want to join the force at all? he wondered. *Life is easy when you're the college boy who gets all the credit. A cop isn't even worth the ink!* Thrusting the magazine away from him in disgust, Nick seethed, his pulse pounding in his ears.

Out of the corner of his eye Nick saw two beat cops enter the diner and sit down in one of the window booths. Nick understood the look of weary pain on their faces. He'd experienced it many times after a particularly grueling stakeout. Who wouldn't get tired? Working odd hours and catching irregular meals was an exhausting way to live.

Nick nodded a sympathetic greeting to the two older cops. As he did so he noticed two slimy-looking thugs walk by the window. Jeering and laughing, they made obscene gestures at the cops. The cops didn't even appear to notice.

What's it all for anyway? Nick asked himself angrily. *Policemen and policewomen give their lives to protect people. They pound the pavement night and day so that the rest of the world can sleep safely. And for what? So two punks can laugh in their faces? So they can retire with a gold watch and barely enough money to make ends meet?*

Who needs it? Nick asked himself with a sigh. Those two creeps flipping the bird had convinced him. It was time for a change. Nick wanted a better life. He wanted to be able to kick back and relax with Jessica without always having to be on call for an emergency.

This is it, he told himself. *I'm going to go back home and prepare for those exams, no matter what it takes. I'm getting into college if it kills me!*

"Jessica! Hey, Jessica! Over here!" Denise waved her straw hat, hoping to catch Jessica's eye through the noise and bustle of downtown Sweet Valley.

"Hey, Denise, what's going on?" Jessica asked, crossing the street to join Denise on the sidewalk. "You look as if you're in a good mood. Any special reason?"

"I guess I *am* feeling pretty good," Denise replied as she replaced her hat at a jaunty angle. But she couldn't help thinking the same couldn't be said of Jessica. Although she looked as beautiful as always, she didn't seem to be her usual cheerful self. "I was just on my way to Tea for Two to get some lunch. Want to come?"

Tea for Two was one of the fanciest places around. It was also one of the prettiest, with Belgian lace curtains, sparkling crystal, and flowers on every table. Denise had always wanted to go there, but she wouldn't have been able to drag Winston along at the end of a rope.

"So *that's* why you're looking so fancy," Jessica said.

"Oh, this is nothing." Denise dismissed her pink polka-dot sundress and strappy sandals with a wave of her hand. "If you think *this* is a nice outfit, just wait until you see the dress I'm getting later today!"

"Uh-huh."

Denise's happy smile turned confused. She had banked on Jessica to get all excited so that Denise would have an excuse to share her plans about buying the gorgeous peach dress she'd seen at Chris and Candies. It just wasn't like Jessica not to care about shopping. Clearly something was very wrong.

She squinted at her friend, searching for some kind of sign. *That's weird*, Denise told herself. *Since when does Jessica wear such heavy, garish makeup?* She looked as if she was wearing an inch of muddy pancake; burgundy stripes had been painted on each cheekbone, and electric blue eyeliner peeked out from under false eyelashes.

"I can see what you're thinking, Denise," Jessica said with a rueful smile. "I just finished doing the calendar shoot with Bobby Hornet, and I haven't had a chance to get all this crud off yet."

"Wow!" Denise breathed, impressed. She hooked her arm through Jessica's, and they began walking toward the café. "So that explains the war paint. Was it fun?"

"Fun?" Jessica groaned. "I've had more fun at the dentist!"

"Oh, please!" Denise blurted as they entered the restaurant. "You loved every minute of it. Just spill."

Tea for Two was mostly empty, and the hostess led them over to a small table near the window. The sun shining through the lace curtains made pretty patterns on the lilac linen tablecloth, and the napkins were folded into an elaborate origami-like design. Denise leaned forward to smell the bouquet of sweetheart roses in a crystal bud vase, then sat back with an air of complete satisfaction.

"Anyway," Denise prompted. "About Bobby Hornet—"

"You're not gonna believe what I saw," Jessica began wearily. "I'm *so* disillusioned. . . ."

"Oooh, what is it? Is it juicy?"

Jessica grabbed the roots of her bizarrely teased blond hair and rolled her eyes dramatically. "Hair extensions! Hel*lo*-o!"

Denise clapped her hands over her mouth. "*Eek!* You're *kidding!* You mean that gorgeous mane is *fake?*"

"As fake as his whole nice-guy act," Jessica began. "He—"

"How are you doing today, ladies," a waitress announced, regarding Jessica and Denise with a tinge of disdain.

The waitress's manner suddenly chilled Denise. But when she remembered the little plastic card tucked away in her purse, her confidence returned. Straightening her spine, she replied, "Fine, thank you, *miss.*"

The waitress replied with a courteous smile. "What may I serve you this afternoon?"

"Hmmm . . . what would you like, Jess?" Denise asked, flipping open her menu.

Jessica barely glanced at the menu before slamming it shut. "I'll have whatever you're having," she muttered.

Denise coolly ordered two iced teas and two orders of tea sandwiches. After the waitress departed with the order, Denise turned to Jessica and looked at her with concern. "Are you OK, Jess? Did Bobby's hair extensions really bother you *that* much?"

"Well, *no.*" Jessica smiled slightly. "But *everything*

about him seems so fake, you know? Like his whole image—it's dishonest in a way. Just like modeling."

"What do you mean?" Denise asked as the waitress brought two tall, frosted glasses of iced tea to the table. Denise added some sweetener to her drink and stirred it with a sterling silver swizzle stick.

"I mean, look at this calendar shoot," Jessica continued bitterly. "Look at *me*. It took *hours* to make me up, and I'm probably going to end up airbrushed anyway. I'm just beginning to think that . . . that the *media* is completely unfair to women, you know? I mean, their expectations are totally unrealistic! No women look perfect in real life. Not even top models!" Jessica's eyes smoldered with anger.

"Excuse me?" Denise spluttered, splattering her iced tea in a completely *un*dainty fashion. "I don't think I heard you correctly. Did you say something about the media being unfair to women?" She collapsed back in her chair and stared at Jessica.

Jessica nodded defiantly. "You got it."

Denise giggled. "OK, now I understand. You're actually *Elizabeth,* and you did one of those twin switcheroo things . . . right?"

"Nope," she replied, squaring her shoulders. "You're talking to Jessica Wakefield, all right. The *new* Jessica Wakefield." She reached for her iced tea and stirred it energetically. "I'm about to make some major changes in my life, Denise. Just watch!"

Denise gazed at Jessica in awe. *What's next?* she wondered. *Is she going to tell me she's becoming a nun?*

"What's the matter?" Jessica asked. "Cat got your tongue?"

"Well, I . . . I'm impressed!" Denise said sincerely, lifting her drink in a toast. She and Jessica clinked glasses as the waitress set down two plates covered with exquisite little tea sandwiches.

"I can't believe that dumb old calendar shoot affected you *that* much," Denise continued, picking up a watercress sandwich. "It must have been quite a trauma."

"It wasn't just the calendar," Jessica said, her finger tracing the delicate pattern of fruits and flowers on the china serving plate. "It was that *NEWS2US* article too. Did you read it? Ugh! That *really* burned me!"

Denise nodded. "Yeah, Jess. I couldn't believe that they didn't mention you or Nick at all. And what about Bruce? I bet Lila's plenty steamed that he didn't get any credit—not to mention Bruce himself. I was totally blown away by it."

"*You* were blown away?" Jessica chewed on the sprig of mint from her glass of iced tea. "Well, then you can imagine how *devastated* I was. And I know it can't be *Elizabeth's* fault—"

"Oh, of course not!" Denise interrupted. "That article totally slammed her!"

Jessica shook her head, a look of disgust on her

face. "My sister is way too classy to sell her friends out like that."

Denise nodded and reached for another tea sandwich.

"You know what the whole thing boils down to?" Jessica asked, her voice tinged with rage.

"What?" Denise asked, blotting her lips with a lilac linen napkin.

"Exactly what I said before," Jessica declared, pounding her fist lightly on the table. "The media is totally unfair to women! We just don't get any respect!"

Denise stared at her friend, slack jawed, stunned at how she seemed to be turning into a completely different person before her very eyes—and it had nothing to do with the garish makeup.

"I mean it, Denise! Look how Scott came off— like some boy wonder! But what about Elizabeth? *She* came off like her only contribution to the story was sharpening Scott's pencils! I mean, you'd never see an article that said something like, 'Cute boy-toy Scott Sinclair is following in his brilliant girlfriend's footsteps.' No way!" Jessica tossed her head angrily. "I'm *tired* of how women are always treated as if they're nothing but *brainless bimbos!* It's time for a change!"

"Amen, sister!" Denise applauded as the waitress brought over the check discreetly folded in half. "Let me get this." She reached into her purse and removed her SVU gold card.

Jessica's eyes widened. "Since when have you carried plastic, Denise?"

"Oh, this old thing?" Denise looked nonchalant. "I don't know. . . . I only use it for special occasions." She signaled the waitress with her card, feeling extremely sophisticated. When the bill was brought back, Denise signed with a flourish, adding an extravagant tip.

Jessica smiled. "Thanks, Denise. I really appreciate this. It was just the pick-me-up I needed after a *really* rotten day!"

Denise waved Jessica's thanks away. "So where are you headed now? Want to hit some shops with me?"

Jessica shook her head. "I'd love to, but I should get back to campus. I haven't seen Elizabeth since the article hit the stands. She's probably bumming big time."

"Give her my best, would you?" Denise said as they gathered their things and walked toward the exit. Her eyes sparkled as she thought of all the beautiful doors just waiting to be opened by her credit card. What was the name of that boutique Lila had mentioned? Claudette's? Lila had gotten a gorgeous pair of silver heels there, and Denise was itching to go and try on a pair herself. But first she had a date with a peach dress, arranged for her by the Only Bank of Gittenbach, New York!

Chapter
Six

If Scott's already heard from DCIR, does that mean I'll be hearing from them soon too? Elizabeth wondered as she stopped in front of the row of mailboxes inside Dickenson Hall. As she fished in her backpack for the tiny metal key, she could see that the box was stuffed to the point of overflowing.

Don't get too excited, she told herself, trying to calm the fluttering in her heart. *It's probably all junk mail.*

Elizabeth quickly swung open the little door of the mailbox. "Let's see . . . a flyer for two-for-one skydiving lessons . . . a boutique announcement for Jess . . . a wrong address . . . a thick envelope from Denver . . . the *Denver Center for Investigative Reporting!* Oh, my gosh, it's *here!*"

Frozen in place, Elizabeth stared down at the heavy, cream-colored envelope with its fancy seal.

Her heart thumped painfully against her ribs. Wasn't it a good sign that the envelope was so thick? Most rejections were just written on a single page, weren't they?

She weighed the envelope in her shaking hands. "Just open it, silly!" Elizabeth muttered to herself. She hesitated a second longer before dashing into the stairwell, out of sight from the other dorm residents milling about in the lobby. She took a deep breath, then two, and then tore into the envelope, pulling out a matching piece of letterhead paper.

"'Dear Ms. Wakefield,'" she read aloud, "'blah, blah, blah, thank you for thinking of us, blah, blah, blah . . .' Well, where does it sayyy . . . *eek!* 'We're proud to extend a warm welcome to you, Ms. Wakefield, and are pleased to announce that we have selected you to enroll in the Denver Center for Investigative Reporting'! I got in! *I got in!* Scott is right. I'm a great reporter!"

Elizabeth glanced through the accompanying materials. There was a glossy brochure with photographs of the campus, a course catalog, and a card that she was supposed to send back indicating her acceptance or refusal of the offer. Gathering her backpack, she rushed up the stairs with renewed energy to tell Jessica.

"Jessica, guess what?" Elizabeth cried as she burst into room 28.

"Hey, Elizabeth," Jessica replied from her bed.

Wrapped in her purple satin comforter, she was eating a bowl of ice cream as she watched the WSVU news on an unfamiliar television set that sat balanced on top of her messy desk. "Check it out. This TV has awesome reception! Kristy was so cool about lending it to us while she's away." She clicked the remote to lower the volume. "Want some ice cream?"

Elizabeth laughed. "Why not?" She put her backpack neatly on her desk chair. Stepping carefully, she picked her way over piles of Jessica's laundry and beauty products to the small refrigerator. "After all, I've got something to celebrate!"

Or do I? Elizabeth thought as she began scooping caramel praline swirl into one of their bright flowered bowls. Seeing Jessica snuggled up in her quilt like a little girl had made Elizabeth realize just how much she would miss her sister if she left.

I never really imagined that I would get into DCIR, she thought. *I didn't even consider the ramifications. If I decide to go, will I be able to handle being away from Jessica for so long?* Elizabeth sighed, her good mood turning slightly sour. *Why can't I just enjoy the fact that I got in and save the heavy decisions for later?*

"Celebrate?" Jessica quirked an eyebrow. "Why do you want to celebrate? Didn't you see the *NEWS2US* article? I thought you'd be wrecked!"

Elizabeth frowned as she remembered the patronizing interview. "I *was* really bent out of shape." Laughing bitterly, Elizabeth kicked off her shoes and settled down on her immaculate pink-and-white bed. "But I just had some good news, and that sort of makes up for it." Elizabeth paused. "I . . . I got accepted into this really good journalism program."

"That's great, Liz," Jessica said absently. Judging from the look on her face, she didn't appear to have heard Elizabeth's announcement.

I guess she's preoccupied, Elizabeth thought, eyeing her sister a little more closely. *She must be upset about the article too. I'll save the details for another time. Besides, I don't want Jess to start worrying about me leaving when I don't even know if I'm going to!*

"I'm sorry, Jess. I completely forgot about you," Elizabeth said contritely. "I know how much you were looking forward to being mentioned. I *did* tell the reporter about your contribution to the investigation, but nothing I said ended up in the magazine." Elizabeth stretched out on her bed and turned toward the TV. She swallowed hard as she saw the face of Tom Watts fill the tiny screen.

He looks so handsome, she thought. *He really has charisma.* In spite of her pain Elizabeth couldn't help but be impressed with Tom's on-camera ability. She couldn't really make out what he was saying—the volume was too low. Still, Elizabeth felt a familiar tug at her heartstrings at the quiet murmuring of his voice.

Jessica put her empty bowl down on her bed and leaned back into her mountain of pillows. "I was really upset, Liz, for all of us. You, me and Nick, even Bruce. I was practically seeing red! Well, I guess you know how I must feel because it was even worse for you—"

"What was that?" Elizabeth interrupted, sitting bolt upright on the edge of the bed. "Could you turn up the volume, please?"

Jessica searched for the remote under the mounds of pillows but only came up with her ice-cream spoon.

"Hurry up!" Elizabeth said impatiently. "I just heard something that sounded like—"

"Got it!" Jessica shouted triumphantly. She pulled the remote out from under the covers and pressed the volume key to max. Elizabeth winced at the roar. "Oops, sorry." Jessica modified the volume, and Tom's rich voice filled the room.

"Questions regarding the appropriateness of Scott Sinclair's interview in *NEWS2US* arose today when it was found that Mr. Sinclair's father sits on the board of Morgan Media Holdings. Morgan Media Holdings is the parent company of *NEWS2US*, leading some to wonder if the flattering profile was due more to family connections than to personal achievement." The serious implications of Tom's report were underscored by the grave look on his face as he spoke.

Elizabeth shook her head, wondering if she'd heard him correctly. "I can't believe it, Jess! That sounds completely unethical. Tom must have his facts wrong!" Deep down, Elizabeth doubted that was the case. Despite what she thought of Tom personally, she knew he was an excellent reporter. Leaning forward, she focused on the broadcast.

"Many insist that Mr. Sinclair is a fine journalist who richly deserves to be interviewed, citing his recent acceptance into the prestigious Denver Center of Investigative Reporting as proof of his abilities. But WSVU was shocked to learn that DCIR's undergraduate journalism program is in fact underwritten by Morgan Media Holdings."

Even though Tom continued speaking, Elizabeth's attention wandered. She was far too upset to concentrate. *If the journalism program is sponsored by MMH and Scott's father sits on the board . . . then what is going on here?* she asked herself uneasily. She jumped up, knocking her empty ice-cream bowl to the floor, and began pacing back and forth.

"Wow, Scott sure sounds as if he's on some kind of inside track." Jessica smirked. "No wonder the article made him sound like a boy wonder!"

"It's incredible, Jess. I mean, the *NEWS2US* article could *maybe* have been a coincidence, but getting into DCIR too? I don't think so," Elizabeth said fiercely.

"Some guys have all the luck, huh?" Jessica quipped.

Seething, Elizabeth picked up the phone and started punching Scott's number with one hand while turning down the TV's volume with the other. "I *can't* wait to hear how Scott worms his way out of this one!" she muttered.

"Ummm . . . I think maybe I'll go take a shower and leave you two alone." Jessica jumped up and grabbed her bathrobe and beauty bag.

Elizabeth looked quizzically at Jessica as she waited for Scott to pick up. It was so unlike Jessica to walk out on an argument that would surely be a juicy gossip item.

Jessica laughed as if she could read Elizabeth's mind. "It's not that I don't want a blow-by-blow description from you later. It's just that from the look on your face, I don't think my eardrums could handle being in the same room with you for the next ten minutes!" Jessica scooped up her shower cap and ran out of the room.

The line finally picked up. "Yo."

"Seen any interesting news programs lately?" Elizabeth asked sarcastically.

"Elizabeth? Is that you?"

"Did you catch the broadcast on WSVU?" Elizabeth challenged harshly.

"Yeah, actually. Man, does this prove that TV

journalism takes a backseat to print or what? The *Gazette* would never run a story this flimsy. I mean, did you really *listen*, Elizabeth? Talk about smoke and mirrors!"

"Is it true?" Elizabeth demanded furiously.

"Is *what* true?" Scott asked. "That my father works for MMH? Yeah, so what? So do about thirty million other people!"

"What about the nepotism charge?" Elizabeth persisted.

"Oh, come on! You mean I can't be interviewed by *NEWS2US* because my father sits on the board? He's about ten thousand miles removed from the day-to-day decisions of the magazine!" Scott snorted with disdain. "Listen, Elizabeth, as far as I'm concerned, Watts isn't just one of the most tenth-rate reporters around, he's also one of the most tenth-rate *people*. It's so clear that this is a personal thing. He's just out to get me."

"Look, Scott, if it was just about *NEWS2US*, I wouldn't be so concerned. But what about the fact that MMH underwrites the undergrad program at DCIR? The two things together make for an awfully big coincidence."

"Elizabeth, you're a journalist. I'm surprised that you could be taken in by such a shallow piece of reporting. Take a bunch of unconnected facts and string them together and you can make *anything* sound convincing! You've seen that happen a million times before."

Elizabeth hesitated. The facts sounded pretty conclusive to her, but she *did* know how facts could get twisted. *I should know,* she reminded herself. *Just look at the NEWS2US article! But could it really be as simple as Scott says? Is Tom really out to get him?*

"My father's been in the media industry his whole life," Scott continued, his voice seething with outrage. "That's how I got interested in reporting. Is he supposed to quit because I applied to a school that his company is affiliated with?"

Elizabeth paused. "I guess not."

"What about the reverse? Are all the children of the thirty million employees worldwide supposed to avoid the news business?" Scott chuckled. "I think you'll have to agree that that sounds pretty ridiculous. What if my father was a doctor and I applied to Harvard Medical School? This is essentially the same thing."

Elizabeth had to admit that put that way, Scott's argument made a lot of sense. Still, she wasn't completely comfortable with his explanation. *NEWS2US* was a fast-paced weekly magazine, but DCIR—that was another story. It was a highly regarded journalism school that accepted only the most qualified applicants. Their admissions board would have had to know of Scott's connections.

And how do I fit into this anyway? The thought

slammed into Elizabeth's head. She remembered how Scott had insisted she apply to the program with him. He had even prestamped the application envelope for her. She never would have even dreamed of applying if Scott hadn't talked her into it.

Am I a part of some huge scam? Elizabeth wondered. Maybe Scott had pulled strings for *her* to get in too. *What did Scott do, tell his father that he wanted his girlfriend to go with him?* Her stomach turned over at the thought. To think that just a few minutes ago, she had been so proud to have been accepted.

"You want to know what I really think is going on here?" Scott asked, his hurt tone breaking through Elizabeth's reverie.

"What?"

"I think you're afraid of your feelings for me, Elizabeth. You keep looking for reasons to dislike me." Scott dropped his voice an octave. "Don't you think I deserve better than that from you?"

Elizabeth flinched, feeling as if she had just been thrown a curveball. She wasn't used to hearing Scott sound so vulnerable, and the sudden change in his tone flustered her. *The case against Scott seems tight, but he does have a point,* she conceded. *I do keep trying to find fault with him. Maybe he really is innocent, but what about* my *acceptance? Was he involved with that somehow?*

"Liz? I'm right, aren't I?" Scott sighed. "Why do you keep pulling away from me?"

Elizabeth took a deep breath. Could she trust Scott? Every time she confronted him with some suspicion, he was always able to explain away her fears. Was he a good guy at heart or just a really great actor?

I'll tell Scott that I got accepted now, she decided suddenly. *If he insists that I go or has a hard time sounding surprised, then I'll know he pulled some strings.*

Gripping the receiver tightly, Elizabeth began to tell Scott her news.

Denise skipped along the street giddily, unhampered by the weight of the many packages she was holding. Somehow all the beautiful things she carried were lightening her step instead of weighing her down. Denise mentally reviewed her purchases with a smile on her face.

The peach dress had still been on the rack at Chris and Candies, and Denise had snatched it up along with two others that she hadn't noticed before. Now the peach dress, the burgundy knit, and the midnight blue chiffon were all snuggled safely in tissue paper and packed into one of Chris and Candies's glossy striped shopping bags. Three dresses were more than Denise was used to buying at one time, but as far as she was concerned, it was just the beginning.

"Let's see," Denise said to herself. "That navy chiffon is a little stark. Maybe it could use a necklace."

Denise crossed the street and went into a fine jewelry store. There were so many beautiful pieces on display, it was hard for her to choose. Should she get the topaz earrings? The turquoise ring? The pearl studs? She casually collected a delicate pair of silver earrings, a gold filigree bracelet, and a fancy diver's watch for Winston before she made her way over to the cash register.

"Will there be anything else?" the salesclerk asked respectfully as she totaled up the bill.

"Oh, how stupid of me!" Denise gave a small shriek. "I came in here for a necklace. Do you have anything with garnets?"

"Right over here." The clerk led the way to a glass display case, and Denise wasted no time in choosing an exquisite teardrop choker. Denise smiled with satisfaction as she added the necklace to her purchases. Still smiling, she handed over her credit card and signed the bill with a flourish. The clerk rushed to open the door for Denise, and she danced happily out onto the street.

Why did I wait so long to get a credit card? she wondered. *This is the most fun I've had in ages, and I've only just started!* Her face fell as she realized she'd only bought Winston one present. *Winnie deserves more than that!* she thought, stopping outside a men's haberdashery. The Italian designer suits in the window were stunning, but she had to admit that none of the fancy clothes on display matched Winston's unique style. A frown creased her brow momentarily but vanished as she entered the store.

When Denise left ten minutes later with two luxurious cashmere sweaters and a red-and-white-striped ascot, she was positively glowing. *Winnie will look so adorable in that ascot!* she thought, laughing aloud as she pictured Winston Egbert in a pair of his trademark baggy overalls and a loud Hawaiian shirt with the ascot around his neck.

Now for those silver shoes that Lila bought! Denise sashayed into Claudette's and plopped herself down in a plush velvet chair. She gasped aloud at the many pairs of shoes on display, each more beautiful than the next. *How can I possibly choose?* she asked herself as a clerk brought over the coveted silver pair. They were stunning, but so were the black strappy sandals and the bone-colored pumps. The heels with the complicated ankle straps would match the navy dress perfectly, but how could she turn down the magenta patent leather mules?

I guess I'll have to get more than one pair, Denise decided with a giggle. *But I don't want to be greedy. I'll draw the line at four!* Sighing happily, Denise followed the clerk over to the register. Along the way she noticed that Claudette's also carried men's shoes, so she requested a pair of ultrachic loafers and a pair of cozy bedroom slippers, both in size eleven. Denise signed and pocketed the receipt, not even bothering to look at the amount. "Now . . . for accessories."

Denise left Claudette's struggling under the weight of the shoe boxes but perked up as she passed a store with an exquisite window display. Gossamer silk scarves were draped gracefully over evening gowns and fancy lingerie. The entire display shrieked luxury and class, and Denise hesitated on the doorstep for a second. "Well, just a few scarves, that's all," Denise said thoughtfully. "A silk blouse, maybe a hat or two, some perfume . . ."

"May I help you, miss?" a tall, chic woman with her hair in a chignon asked as Denise entered the store. She was dressed all in black, and her makeup was elegant and subtle. "Are you just looking?" she inquired with a faint French accent. She sniffed and flicked a nonexistent piece of dust off the sleeve of her dress. Until today she was exactly the type of saleswoman who had always intimidated Denise, but not any longer!

"Hmmm? Excuse me?" Denise paused as she was trying on a black hat with an enormous ostrich feather. "Just looking? Oh no. Today I'm *buying!*"

"Elizabeth, that's wonderful news! I'm so happy for you! When did you find out?" Scott's voice rang across the phone lines with bright enthusiasm that contrasted sharply with the hurt tone heard only moments before.

He certainly sounds surprised, Elizabeth thought, crossing over to the window. The sky had turned cloudy—a perfect match for her thoughts. *But what if he pressures me to go? Let's see what he has to say about that!*

Elizabeth cleared her throat nervously. "So . . . do you think I should accept?"

"You know I would never try and give you advice about such an important decision," Scott said seriously. "That's for you to figure out. I'm sure that whatever you decide will be the best thing for you. Just remember." Scott's voice deepened. "You should feel really proud. I'm really proud . . . of both of us."

"Thank you, Scott," Elizabeth said quietly. *He sounds so genuine,* she thought. *Like he truly wants what's best for me.*

"I'll let you go," he continued. "I know you have a lot of important decisions to make, and you probably want to be left alone."

"Thanks. That's exactly what I need right now."

"Then I'll catch up with you later. Bye, Liz."

Elizabeth sat down, the phone dangling limply from her hand. She felt oddly frustrated. *What's wrong with me?* she asked herself. *Scott acted like a perfect gentleman, and I'm disappointed!*

"Maybe he's right," she said with a groan. "Maybe I *am* just looking for reasons to push him away." She hung up the phone with a sigh and turned up the volume on the TV again.

WSVU was still broadcasting, but the program had moved on to other news. Elizabeth looked at Tom. Right now all that was visible of him was the back of his head as he interviewed a student about her recent award-winning science project. Elizabeth grabbed a pillow and hugged it to herself forlornly. She watched as Tom expertly questioned his guest. The student was somewhat shy and noncommunicative, but Tom drew her out until she was fairly sparkling with enthusiasm. *Tenth-rate journalist, my foot!* she thought defensively. *Tom's an excellent journalist!*

Elizabeth wandered over to her desk and took out her journal. She needed some time to sort out her thoughts, and with Jessica in the shower she could write freely. But instead of writing she flipped through the pages slowly. She smiled as she read some of her earliest entries at SVU. *I've changed so much since college began,* she thought proudly.

When she first started college, Elizabeth had had a difficult time. Things had started going wrong when she broke up with Todd Wilkins, her longtime high-school boyfriend. As if that weren't bad enough, she'd also had a falling-out with her closest friend, Enid Rollins, who had changed her name to Alexandra and turned into a boisterous party girl.

I was so lonely back then, Elizabeth recalled. With no friends to turn to, Elizabeth had turned to food—and had gained the dreaded "freshman fifteen." For a while it had seemed as if Elizabeth Wakefield, former golden girl, was on a fast track to nowhere.

But that was before she had started working at WSVU. WSVU had been her salvation. She'd immersed herself in learning the demanding craft of broadcast journalism. She'd reveled in the challenges of a medium that was much more collaborative than print. It had been a new experience for Elizabeth, who had only worked with her word processor before, to give direction to a video crew or to listen patiently while a member of the camera crew explained why a shot wouldn't work. It had been an intense, invigorating time, and through it all there had been Tom.

Tom. Elizabeth felt a bittersweet pang as she read over her first impressions of Tom Watts. She'd been impressed by his abilities as a newsman, shy about her feelings for him, and wildly attracted to him. From the very beginning there had been a chemistry between the two of them that had been impossible to deny.

Things hadn't been such smooth sailing at the start of their relationship, though. Elizabeth and Tom had each been unsure of the other's feelings. It wasn't until after they'd investigated a fraternity hazing prank together that they had admitted their love for each other. The triumph of solving the case had been almost as exciting as their love. Elizabeth would always remember the exhilaration that she had felt with Tom at the conclusion of a successful story. *I certainly have never felt that way working with Scott,* Elizabeth realized.

Her mind drifted back to the time she and Tom had finally cracked SVU's secret society, when Tom had told her he loved her. Elizabeth shuddered as she remembered their first kiss. She couldn't believe that she had captured the heart of someone so brilliant, so gorgeous.

Blinking back tears, Elizabeth looked up at the TV screen, where Tom had turned back to face the camera. Even now Elizabeth couldn't help admiring his dark hair, his deep brown eyes, and the build that had made him a football superstar. *Tom looks like such a* man, she mused. *Scott's more of a pretty boy.*

"Oh, why do I keep comparing them? It's not *fair!*" Elizabeth pounded her fist on her desk in frustration. "It's not as if Scott is all bad . . . and Tom Watts certainly isn't all *good!*" She gave a ragged sigh, remembering how much Tom had hurt her.

I thought that nothing could feel worse than having Tom's father come on to me, but I was wrong. Nothing felt worse than having Tom disbelieve me! Elizabeth closed her eyes, replaying the painful scenes that had ended their relationship. She remembered how he had accused her of being jealous of his new family, how he had called her a liar.

She still hurt deep inside, but it was no longer the sharp anguish that it had been at first. Now it was clouded over with a thousand other feelings and memories. For every argument that wounded Elizabeth, the memory of a sweet romantic gesture helped to heal her. She couldn't forget the horrible things he'd said to her, but she couldn't forget the beautiful poems he'd written her either.

A tear crept down Elizabeth's cheek. *There's only one thing I know for sure—that I'm completely confused! Can I really leave SVU forever when I'm so unsure of my feelings? No. I have to see Tom again. Just one more time. Then I'll know how I really feel!*

Chapter Seven

"Did anyone here get a chance to check out that new Sigma?" Mandy Carmichael gushed. "He's absolutely gorgeous!"

Jessica sighed deeply as she tried to tune out the excited chatter of the Thetas. As much as Jessica loved her sorority sisters, she wasn't in the mood for dishing about the newest member of the Sigmas or hearing about the latest cellulite creams. In fact, there were a lot of things she would rather be doing on a sunny Tuesday afternoon than hanging out at Theta house. Unfortunately Alison Quinn, the snooty vice president, had called a meeting, and attendance was mandatory. Even worse, Alison was already fifteen minutes late.

I'm sure I'll be stuck here for hours! Jessica thought. She reached into her purse and dug out her nail file. *I might as well get some work done while I wait.*

"Hey, Jess, do you want me to do that for you?" Isabella called out. Isabella often held marathon manicure sessions at Theta house.

"I'd be honored," Jessica replied, moving over to where Isabella was sitting with all her paraphernalia. "Hey, does anyone know why Alison called this meeting?"

"You mean you don't *know?*" Mandy shrilled, her eyebrows arched in surprise.

"No. Is it *momentous?*" Jessica asked, feeling a mild flutter of interest. "Did Alison finally discover an antidote for her limp, lifeless locks or something?"

"I heard that we're going to get a glimpse of your proofs from the calendar shoot," Denise answered.

"Oh." Jessica's interest vanished. Idly she watched as Isabella began applying a pale pink polish to her nails with smooth, even strokes.

"Guess what, girls?" the reedy voice of Alison Quinn trilled as she pranced into the lounge, her bony hips sashaying back and forth. As always, Tina Chai and Kimberly Schuyler shadowed her every move. Alison waltzed to the center of the room and waved a portfolio at them. "Do you know what I've got in here?" she simpered.

"Let me guess—the proofs from the photo shoot," Jessica replied, deadpan. "I just can't wait."

Alison's face fell. "You could try and sound a *little* more enthusiastic, Jessica," she snapped.

125

"After all, *some* people would think that you're *very* fortunate at having been chosen to represent the Thetas."

"Jealous much, Alison?" Lila whispered.

A smile tugged at the corners of Jessica's mouth. Alison had gone all out in her quest to become the Theta chosen to pose with Bobby Hornet in the calendar. Jessica had felt a small thrill of spiteful satisfaction when she had been chosen instead. *But that was before,* Jessica thought, remembering the boredom of the photo shoot. *I couldn't care less now.*

"Well anyway," Alison continued sourly. "I've had a chance to see the proofs, and I have to say, Jessica, that you don't look bad. Not bad at all."

"Oh, puh-*leeze,*" Isabella called out. "Jessica must look fabulous. Why do you think Bobby chose her over yo—um . . . the rest of us?"

Alison didn't say anything as she handed the portfolio to Kimberly. She and Tina started tacking up the proofs.

"Oooh, Jessica, you look *awesome,*" Denise breathed.

"Fantastic," Mandy chimed in.

Suddenly the air was filled with the approving chatter of all the Thetas as they rushed forward, Jessica included, and admired the proofs.

"Aren't you proud?" a new pledge named Clarissa gushed.

Jessica shuddered as she examined the shots.

She had to admit that she looked great, but she also looked naked. *Nick was right,* she thought with a pang. *There's nothing classy about a bikini calendar. Nothing at all!*

Feeling exposed and embarrassed, Jessica backed away from the throng. "I'm not doing it," she announced quietly. "Get rid of those pictures. I don't want to be in the calendar."

Dead silence greeted her pronouncement.

"What?" Alison finally shrieked. "Are you saying you're quitting, Jessica Wakefield?" she continued in an icy tone. "Because if you are, I'm going to have to seriously question your commitment to the Thetas—or your commitment to anything else, for that matter!"

"That's not fair, Alison," Lila defended. "If Jessica doesn't want to be involved, she has every right." Despite her pronouncement Lila still looked surprised.

"If Jessica quits, will Theta house still be represented?" Clarissa asked.

"Well, I'm sure that Bobby won't be *too* surprised by this turn of events," Alison declared nastily. "He must have seen enough of Jessica to know that she's *totally* unreliable. In any case, I intend to show true Theta spirit and offer to pose instead."

I won't even dignify that with a reply, Jessica told herself. *I know I'm doing the right thing.*

"What about the rest of us? Can we audition too?" Mandy asked.

127

An excited buzz filled the room.

"I want to try," Tina Chai called out.

"What about me?" Mandy asked. "I've been working out with this hot new personal trainer. He works with *all* the stars, and he says that my body is as good as any of theirs!"

Lila snickered. "How much are you paying him to say that?"

"I really think *I* should be the one who's chosen." Alison raised her voice above the babble. "After all, I would have been Bobby's choice if Jessica hadn't . . ."

Jessica didn't stay around to hear the rest of Alison's blather. She'd had enough. Slinging her jacket over her shoulder, she walked out of the lounge.

Pausing on the steps of Theta house, she took a calming breath. What should she do now? She was feeling depressed and aimless. Should she see if Elizabeth was free? Should she go to a movie? Should she call Nick?

Nick. Jessica's heart skittered against her ribs as the image of his handsome face floated before her. She missed talking to him. She missed kissing him. She missed *him*. They hadn't hooked up in days.

Not since that horrible argument, Jessica realized. Sure, she and Nick had had plenty of arguments in the past. In fact, Nick always joked that he wouldn't love her as much without her fiery temper. Jessica grinned, remembering the affectionate way she and Nick usually made up after a fight. Nick always called her within twenty-four hours at the latest. They'd never gone this long without making up!

Why hasn't he called? she wondered, kicking a stone in her path. Had she hurt him too much the other night? Had he decided to call it quits? Jessica longed for the comfort of Nick's arms. She wanted to tell him that he was right about the calendar shoot. She wanted to apologize for her crack about him not being book-smart.

But what if it's too late? Jessica thought miserably. *What if he hasn't called because he's met someone else? Or what if . . .*

Jessica stopped dead in her tracks, her heart pounding uncomfortably. What if Nick didn't call because he *couldn't?* What if he was in trouble? Injured? Maybe he was in the hospital! Or even worse, maybe at this moment Nick was lying wounded somewhere, unable to move, calling for her!

And I tried to talk him out of quitting the police! she thought wretchedly. *I didn't want him to do something nice and safe!* An image of Nick, his body battered and bleeding, filled her mind.

What if Nick wasn't even wounded?

What if he was . . . *dead?*

Terrified, Jessica broke into a run.

Elizabeth stood on the grassy hill that over-looked the WSVU building. From her post she

129

could see into the window of Tom's office. She knew he was there. But even though Elizabeth had every intention of going in and talking to him, she couldn't bring herself to cross the last fifteen yards that separated them.

"What am I so nervous about? He's not going to bite me, is he?" Elizabeth asked a butterfly that settled on her hand. "No," she said soberly. "He won't bite me, but he could hurt me again." The butterfly flew away.

Elizabeth sat down on the grass and hugged her knees to her chest. Somehow, underneath the warm sun, the conviction that she had to talk to Tom was evaporating into a swirl of nervousness. "What's wrong with me?" Elizabeth asked herself. "We're both two mature, reasonable adults. There's no reason why I can't just go in and have a perfectly rational conversation with him."

But Elizabeth knew that she was too keyed up emotionally to have a calm discussion. "Maybe I should wait until I'm feeling a little more confident. Maybe I should go home and change. Maybe I should call the whole thing off."

Elizabeth shook her head at her indecisiveness but remained steadfastly where she was. She was sure that she was doing the right thing. All she needed was a few more minutes to gear up.

Just a few more minutes. No more than ten. Well, no more than another fifteen. Definitely within the hour!

She wiped her palms, which were sweating slightly, on her legs. "Did I wear the right thing?" she murmured fretfully, looking down at her denim-clad thighs. As far as she knew there was no set dress code for how you were supposed to look when seeing old boyfriends, but she wanted to look special. Elizabeth had spent at least twenty minutes changing in and out of clothes that morning, unsure of what to wear, putting on one outfit only to take it off five minutes later. She had scrounged frantically in Jessica's many cosmetic cases for some extra makeup but had scrubbed it all off anyway when she saw how foolish she looked. In the end she decided to get dressed in what she would have worn anyway, Tom or no Tom. But now, sitting on the grassy knoll in her overalls and flowered camp shirt, with just a touch of mascara and lip gloss, she couldn't help wishing she'd worn something a *little* more glamorous.

Elizabeth adjusted the bill on her baseball cap and squinted at Tom's window, trying to make out what he was doing inside. He seemed to be pacing back and forth. Elizabeth smiled. Tom had always done that during their long brainstorming sessions. She recognized it as a sign that he was thinking deeply.

I'll just wait until he sits down, Elizabeth told herself. *He's much too preoccupied now. He wouldn't be able to focus on anything I said to him. As soon as he sits down, the minute he stops pacing, I'll run down the hill into his office.*

131

She caught her breath as Tom sat down abruptly.

"OK." Elizabeth gulped. "He needs time to relax now. He's worn out with all that thinking. If I rush in there now, he'll be too tired to hear what I have to say. As soon as he gets up again I'll know that he's refreshed. That'll be my opportunity."

Elizabeth broke off a blade of grass and started chewing on it. She began to hum a tune. As time went on she began to feel slightly more sure of herself, especially because Tom appeared to be taking a catnap. Elizabeth just *knew* that by the time he woke up, she'd be more than ready to talk to him.

She lay down on the grass, her hands clasped behind her head, mentally rehearsing what she would say to Tom. She cleared her throat and deepened her voice. "Tom, we're both mature adults, and I think that the time has come for us to put aside our differences."

"No. Way too formal," she said to herself.

"Hey, Tom. What's up?" she chirped in her best party girl voice.

Nuh-uh. Way too casual.

"Tom, I have something to tell you," Elizabeth announced like a trial lawyer declaiming her closing argument.

Forget it.

Elizabeth sat up abruptly as she felt something brush her foot. "What the . . . ?"

Dana Upshaw stared down at Elizabeth, a nasty

little smile on her face, and continued walking. Although she didn't say anything, animosity radiated out from her body like a halo. She pranced down the hill, her tight black leather jeans and kooky patterned purple crop top clinging to every curve as if spray painted on. Her straw hat, which would have looked more appropriate at a bridal shower, bobbed uncertainly with each step she took.

She certainly gives new meaning to the words fashion victim! Elizabeth thought angrily. *But more important . . . did Dana overhear me?* Her cheeks burned at the thought. She felt about as glamorous as Huck Finn in her baggy overalls as she watched the admiring stares that Dana got from two guys exiting the building.

Angrily she pulled the stalk of grass from her teeth. *Well, I guess I won't have to practice what to say to Tom after all,* Elizabeth thought sadly. *He's made his choice perfectly clear. Wildman Watts and Dangerous Dana. A match made in heaven! If Dana Upshaw is the kind of girl he really likes, fine. It was never meant to work out between us anyway.*

Elizabeth stood up, her eyes burning with unshed tears, and marched to the nearest pay phone. At least there was *one* guy at SVU she could count on. And he certainly didn't have the bad taste to appreciate a girl who paired garden party hats with Hell's Angel jeans!

Tom paced back and forth, his mind teeming

with unanswered questions about Elizabeth. *Didn't she see my report?* he wondered anxiously. He'd been so sure that she would have contacted him after his exposé on Sinclair that he'd barely been able to close his eyes all night. At first he'd thought that she'd give him a call after the broadcast had aired. When he didn't hear from her, he consoled himself with the thought that she was probably busy confronting Scott.

That's why she isn't calling, Tom had thought with satisfaction. *I bet she's really letting Sinclair have it!*

He'd half expected to see her waiting at the office when he came in. When that hadn't happened, he'd sat impatiently by the phone. Each time it rang, he'd snatched up the receiver only to be disappointed.

Finally, worn out by his constant pacing, Tom collapsed on the beat-up old couch. He was just about to doze off when he felt a pair of hands caress his shoulders. *Elizabeth,* he hoped. But his heart sank when he opened his eyes to see Dana smiling seductively at him.

"Oh. Hi, Dana," Tom said gruffly. He raised his eyebrows slightly at her extreme outfit. When they'd first started dating, Tom had thought Dana's clothes were a perfect reflection of her creative, slightly wild personality. But now he couldn't help thinking that Elizabeth wouldn't wear something so, so . . .

Trashy. Go ahead and admit it, pal. Tom got up from the couch and moved over to his desk chair, hoping to avoid her embrace.

"Hi, Tom," Dana purred, following him. She stood behind his chair and began to rub his neck.

Tom closed his eyes, unable to resist. He was stiff and tense, and her soothing hands seemed to work miracles. But as much as he wanted to lean back and relax into the warmth of her massaging hands, he just couldn't. His mind was too filled with thoughts of Elizabeth.

Dana must have sensed him stiffen because she dropped her hands and moved in front of his chair. "What's wrong, Tom?" she asked with a pout, tossing her mane of mahogany curls with an irritated gesture.

Tom couldn't help but admire the way her silken hair swirled about her shoulders when she did that. *She really is beautiful,* Tom told himself. *Trashy clothes or not. Why can't I just let myself enjoy being with her? Why do I keep torturing myself with memories of Elizabeth?*

"Sorry," Tom replied curtly. "I've just had a really hard day. I'm wrecked, and you took me by surprise." He avoided meeting her eyes, sure that if he did so, she would see right through his flimsy explanation.

But Dana only nodded, seemingly satisfied by Tom's answer. She sat down in a chair near him, crossing her Dr. Marten boots casually. Her face took on a thoughtful expression. "So," she drawled, twirling a curl around one finger. "I caught your broadcast last night, Tom. That Scott guy really sounds as if he could teach politicians a thing or two about being slimy. I wonder what Elizabeth sees in him?"

Tom clenched his fists under the desk but didn't say anything.

"I guess she didn't see your broadcast, Tom. I mean, any decent girl who found out about what kind of guy Scott *really* was would be down here on her knees in two seconds thanking you for opening her eyes to the light."

Tom only lifted his shoulders with a tiny shrug, purposely keeping his face expressionless.

"So did Elizabeth thank you?" Dana persisted.

"I haven't heard from her," Tom said tightly. He pulled some papers out of the top drawer and started sorting through them.

Dana suddenly jumped up and ran to the wastebasket, from which she plucked the crumpled issue of *NEWS2US*. "Oh, I've wanted to see this, but I just haven't been able to find a copy *anywhere*." Dana smoothed down the cover. "It was all sold out. I guess this was a popular issue."

"Look, Dana, I've already read the article. If you want the magazine, take it with you," Tom hinted strongly. He waited for Dana to make her good-byes, but after a moment it became clear that she had no intention of leaving. "I'm really busy now. Can I call you later?"

Dana turned the pages of the magazine as if she hadn't heard a word that Tom had said. She walked over to his chair and perched on the corner of the desk. "Wow, they sure make a good-looking couple, don't they?" She held the magazine out at arm's length so that Tom was forced to look at the picture. "They really look as if they belong together. They're both so blond and blue-eyed." Dana made *blond* and *blue-eyed* sound like *boring* and *dull*. "Of course *some* people would say that *we* make a stunning couple too, Tom. We're both so dark and mysterious looking." Dana ran a hand playfully through Tom's hair.

Tom hardly noticed. He was completely fixated on the picture. *Dana's right. They do look like the perfect couple. Did we ever look that right together?*

"You know, it's not just that they're good-looking either," Dana said pensively. "They really seem to have a *connection*. I mean, look at the way Elizabeth is staring at Scott. She positively *adores* him!"

Tom grabbed the magazine out of Dana's hands and studied the picture at close range. *All this time I was so focused on how badly the article slammed Elizabeth,* he thought, noticing once more the loving sparkle in Elizabeth's eyes. *I just totally phased out the picture. How could I have blocked on it? She does look like she adores him!* Tom swallowed hard. *There's no faking that kind of emotion.*

"I guess she loves him enough to overlook his questionable ethics," Dana continued. "That's *so* romantic." She sighed as if truly touched by Elizabeth's devotion. Her words struck Tom like a blow.

Elizabeth *was* sticking by Scott. Tom had showed her who Scott really was, and she didn't care. Tom was sure now that she'd seen the broadcast. *The only reason she hasn't showed up is she isn't going to,* he realized painfully.

"In some ways it makes you wonder just how honest Elizabeth Wakefield is," Dana added, her eyebrows raised.

"Huh?" Tom looked up, noticing Dana for the first time in minutes. He saw how beautiful she was, how vibrant, how *present. Elizabeth's obviously going on with her life,* Tom told himself. *I should just get on with mine too. Why should I break my heart pining for Elizabeth? It's time to move on.*

Decisively Tom reached for Dana and pulled her into his arms. She fell willingly onto his lap and wriggled, settling herself comfortably against his broad chest. The way Dana's hands seductively caressed the muscles of his shoulders and back was incredible.

Who needs Elizabeth Wakefield? Tom thought savagely as he lowered his mouth to Dana's. She seemed to melt underneath him, molding herself to the contours of his body. *By the time I'm done kissing Dana, I won't even be able to remember*

Elizabeth's name.

Never mind Elizabeth, Tom thought with a moan as Dana returned his kiss with a force that shook him. *I won't even remember my own name!*

"Nick! Nick! Open up!" Jessica cried as she pounded frantically on the door to Nick's apartment.

Please be here, she prayed, holding back sobs. *Just answer the door. Nick, I'll do anything....*

"Nick!" Jessica beat on the door with renewed force. Where was he? Why wasn't he answering?

The door opened, and Jessica fell inside—and into Nick's arms. His handsome face had never looked so good to her. Even though she was overwhelmed with relief, she couldn't stop her tears from finally spilling over.

He's safe! He's home and he's safe! I'll never leave him again, Jessica vowed as she held on to her boyfriend more tightly than she ever had before. *If anything had happened, I would have blamed myself!* She snuggled against Nick's muscular chest and sighed.

Nick stroked her hair. "Is something wrong, Jess?"

"Not now," Jessica murmured, raising her tear-stained face to look at him. "But I was so scared. Oh, Nick, I was so scared!"

"Did something happen to you? Did someone hurt you or ..."

Jessica shook her head. "No, nothing happened to me. But Nick, you haven't called me in *days*. I thought something terrible had happened to *you!*" Jessica's blue-green eyes filled with tears again as she replayed the horrible visions of the past hour. "I kept imagining you wounded . . . dying, even!"

"Oh, Jessica, baby. I'm really sorry I haven't called. I know I should have, but I just was too busy. Besides, it hasn't been that long." Nick returned her hug with equal force.

"Nick Fox!" Jessica shrieked. "What's wrong with you! Its been *days!*" Her anxiety vanished as she broke out of the embrace and glared at Nick, her hands on her hips. Now that she knew he was safe and sound, she was angry. As far as Jessica was concerned, being wounded was the *only* acceptable reason Nick could have for not calling her. *Too busy* definitely didn't cut it! He'd been home this whole time with the phone an arm's length away and he hadn't even bothered to pick it up? Major explanations were in order.

If he had a really excellent reason, like he was paralyzed, I might forgive him, Jessica thought. *If he was paralyzed* and *he sent me ten dozen roses.*

"Just *what* have you been so busy with? Or should I say, *who* have you been so busy with?" She peered around the apartment, half expecting to see another woman there.

"I'm really sorry," Nick mumbled apologetically. "I guess I didn't even realize that it had been

140

that long since we'd spoken. I've been so wrapped up in stuff." He gestured vaguely, waving his hands around the apartment, then running them through his hair until it stood on end.

Just what is going on here? Jessica fumed silently. *Nick doesn't call in days, and when I show up, he acts as if he has better things to do! He should be down on his knees begging my forgiveness!*

"All right. I want some answers here." Jessica crossed her arms over her chest.

"So do I." Nick nodded thoughtfully. "Do you have any idea what the root of the word *eleemosynary* is?"

"Whaaat?" Jessica shook her head as if she hadn't heard him correctly. *Maybe this is all some kind of joke,* she told herself. But Nick didn't look like he was joking. He looked right through Jessica and padded back to the dining room. Nick took a sip from a mug, put on a pair of glasses Jessica had never seen before, and began leafing through one of the many books on the table. "I've been trying to find the answer to that for hours."

Jessica looked at Nick in astonishment as she followed him into the dining room. *Is he drunk?* she wondered, picking up his mug and sniffing it with suspicion. *This isn't alcohol; it's chamomile tea!* Jessica slammed it down, dumbstruck. The only person she knew who drank chamomile tea was Elizabeth!

Wondering if he was sick, she walked over and put her hand on his forehead. *Maybe I should call a doctor,* she thought, looking around to see where Nick had put his cordless phone. As she did so she took in the state of the room. Books were piled everywhere from the floor to the ceiling. It looked as if Nick had robbed the SVU library. Empty, overturned Chinese food cartons were scattered here and there, and old coffee cups littered the table.

Jessica gasped. *This place looks as if* I've *been living here!* she mused. *Nick is usually so neat!*

"Nick, what happened here?" Jessica asked, worried.

"Hmmm?" Nick didn't look up. It was as if he couldn't bear to tear himself away from the book he was reading.

"What's going on?" Jessica shrieked with impatience.

"Here it is!" Nick cried excitedly.

"What?" Jessica jumped. The sudden burst of energy that electrified Nick had startled her.

"The derivation of *eleemosynary.* The original root of the word is—"

"Have you gone crazy?" Jessica interrupted.

"Huh? Oh, I know what you're thinking. I don't really need to know the derivation. But I feel it really helps to remember the *definition* of a word if you know the *derivation.* . . ." Nick trailed off as he bent to study the book again.

"Nick, I don't care about elemystery."

"Eleemosynary."

"Whatever. Could you please tell me what's going on here?"

Nick finally raised his head and looked at Jessica. His glasses slid down his nose a little. "I've been studying," he said simply, as if that explained everything. "I've been going over vocabulary words for the college entrance exams. I guess I lost track of time."

Jessica's jaw dropped open. She'd been worrying that he was out getting shot at, and he'd been home . . . *drinking chamomile tea and studying vocabulary words?*

Nick took a sip from his mug and knit his brows over the notes he was reading. She'd never seen him like this before. He was wearing a striped bathrobe and fuzzy socks. He looked a far cry from the man she had fallen in love with. *That* guy looked slightly dangerous, with a leather jacket and a definite attitude. This guy looked, well . . . he looked *adorable*. The slightly preppy-style horn-rimmed glasses made him look like an extra-cute professor—smart, studious, and *safe*.

Jessica shuddered as she remembered the terror of the past hour. She never wanted to live through that kind of panic again. *If something happened to Nick, I'd die! Why did I ever want him to stay on the force?* Jessica wondered suddenly. *If he wants to give it up, why should I pressure him to stay?* A wave

143

of guilt engulfed her. *If he got wounded, it would be because of me!*

Being the girlfriend of a law student suddenly seemed much more attractive than being the girlfriend of a gun-toting cop who had to dodge bullets all day. *I could get used to having a law student boyfriend. So it's not as exciting as police work—so what? As far as I'm concerned, if Nick wants to stay home and bake cookies all day, that's fine with me! As long as he's safe, what does it matter?* She shuddered as she remembered the horrible images that she'd had of Nick, lying bleeding . . . wounded. . . .

Jessica reached for Nick and gave him as crushing a hug as her slender arms could manage.

"Hey, what's all this?" Nick pulled away from Jessica.

"You've been working so hard. Don't you think you deserve a little reward?" Jessica softly kissed Nick on the cheek. "I know how much getting into school means to you. I'm going to help you study in any way I can . . . but right now I'm going to give you a study *break* that you'll never forget!"

Chapter Eight

Out of the frying pan into the fire! Elizabeth thought with a silent laugh. Now that she had some time to think about it, running *toward* Scott after running *away* from Tom didn't seem like the best idea. *But it's too late to back out now,* Elizabeth thought as she dodged the students sitting on the wide stone steps of the library and hurried through the entrance doors. Elizabeth flashed her ID toward the guard and hurriedly punched the elevator button. She didn't want to be late for her meeting with Scott.

Elizabeth stepped off the elevator and onto the third floor. *It's deserted here,* she thought as she looked around at the musty stacks. Shivering slightly, she wrapped her arms tightly around herself. It was rumored that several ghosts dwelt on the third floor. The seemingly endless shelves of books was the perfect spot to harbor a ghost.

It was so quiet, it was almost . . . eerie.

Feeling a little nervous, Elizabeth quickened her pace. *I wonder why Scott wanted to meet here,* she thought. She had to admit that the stacks had a certain atmosphere. *It's so peaceful here and private. . . . In fact, it's kind of romantic.* Elizabeth looked at the rows of leather-bound books with new appreciation. *It's like a set from a gothic movie.*

"Liz," Scott called out, interrupting her reverie. "Over here."

Elizabeth saw Scott standing with his back against the shelves. Even in the dim light of the stacks his blue eyes stood out with startling clarity. Their crystalline depths lit up as she approached him.

"What did you want to see me about?" Scott asked, his voice a warm caress in the silence of the stacks. "Not that I'm not always glad to see you, but you sounded kind of stressed."

"What's that book?" Elizabeth asked irrelevantly, her heart fluttering with uncertainty. It had seemed like such a good idea to talk over her decision with Scott. But now that she was with him, she felt flustered. *Why am I asking him?* she thought. *After all, I have to decide for myself.*

"This?" Scott closed the book that he'd been leafing through. "Nothing, really. Just something to pass the time until you showed." He gave her an intimate smile. "So, you want to talk about the program?"

146

Here it comes, Elizabeth thought. *The ninety-five-mile-an-hour pitch!*

"Well, I can't make your decision for you," Scott said calmly. "That kind of decision is one that only *you* can make. What if I told you to go, and you hated it? What if I told you to stay, and you ended up hating *that?* No sirree." Scott shook his head with a laugh. "You're on your own with this one."

Elizabeth was stunned. She'd been so sure that Scott would pressure her into attending the program with him. Instead he seemed completely low-key.

"I'll tell you how I *can* help you." Scott took her hand, and they began walking slowly through the empty stacks. They were alone except for the thousands of books surrounding them. Even the air was quiet. Small dust particles floated past them, illuminated by patches of sunlight that streamed from the high, mullioned windows.

"How?" Elizabeth asked, her hand relaxing in his. For once holding his hand felt like the *right* thing to do.

"By being your friend, Liz," Scott said simply. "In lots of ways I feel as if I don't really know you at all. We've worked together, sure, and I know that there's something more between us. . . . But even with all that, there's so little we know about each other. Stop me if I'm being presumptuous, but you're facing an important decision right now. . . . You probably need as many friends as you can get." Scott looked down at her with compassion as he squeezed her hand gently. His concern for Elizabeth showed plainly in his face.

He's right, Elizabeth realized with a jolt. *Who else can I talk to about this? I don't want to talk about it with Jess yet—not until I have a better idea of whether I'm going to accept or not. She'll be too upset about the possibility of my leaving to be any help, and Tom's certainly not there for me anymore.*

"Well." Elizabeth nervously cleared her throat. "I—I do think of you as a friend, Scott."

"Then let me *be* a friend." Scott's smile was mischievous. "Tell me what gets you going. Do you only eat the inside of Oreos or the whole cookie? Do you like the old Star Treks or the new ones? Do you think there will ever be a female president or that people will ever live in space? Let me in on what's inside your head."

Elizabeth couldn't help laughing. "Well, I don't like Oreos at all, but I can eat a whole bag of chocolate-chip cookies at one sitting. The old Star Treks, definitely—I can't even watch the new ones. A female president? I sure hope so! And as far as people living in space . . . that sounds like science fiction. But look at our grandparents; they probably thought that landing on the moon was science fiction."

Scott looked upset. "Elizabeth, I don't know how to tell you this. . . ."

Did I say something wrong? Elizabeth wondered.

Scott cleared his throat. "If you don't like Oreos, then we probably *can't* be friends," he finished solemnly.

Elizabeth punched Scott lightly on the arm. They had stopped walking and were standing near one of the little tables that were scattered throughout the stacks. Elizabeth leaned back against the table and shifted her backpack to the floor.

"Seriously, Liz, tell me what goes on in that beautiful head of yours," Scott said quietly.

Elizabeth smiled slightly. "These days I don't seem to know myself. I used to be so sure of what I wanted. . . ."

"And what was that?"

"To be a good journalist. OK, let's be honest. A *great* journalist. A Pulitzer Prize winner." Elizabeth blushed slightly, surprised at how much she was revealing to Scott.

"And now?" Scott's voice was soft as he tucked a strand of Elizabeth's silky blond hair behind her ear.

"I still want to be a great journalist," Elizabeth said with conviction. She tilted her head to one side. "But I don't know what that means anymore. Does it mean staying at SVU? Does it mean going away? I know that the other school is more prestigious, but is it necessarily better? Even if it is better, will it be better for *me*? Maybe being away from my

149

sister would make my work suffer, or maybe it would make us both grow more." Elizabeth shrugged. "I just don't know, Scott."

"Sounds like you have some heavy thinking ahead of you," Scott said. "It means a lot that you've opened up to me this much, Elizabeth. For such a long time now I've felt as if you've been pushing me away."

"I'm sorry." Elizabeth felt her face redden. She was glad that the light in the stacks was too dim to reveal her blush. Elizabeth was surprised at how easily their conversation had turned to writing, and how hands-off Scott had been about the whole thing. Smiling, Elizabeth turned to look Scott head-on. She was startled to see that his face was so close to hers, his full lips just inches from her own, his blue eyes looking into hers with amazing intensity.

"Elizabeth," Scott murmured. He lowered his mouth to hers. His kiss was warm and gentle at first. When Elizabeth put her arms around him, he deepened it, pressing her close to him.

She felt herself melting, her insides turning to butter at the way Scott held her. Elizabeth returned Scott's kiss enthusiastically as he tightened his clasp on her waist. She tingled from her head to her toes as she reached up to run her hands through Scott's hair. His arms felt muscular and strong around her, and he smelled a little of cologne—not like Tom, who always smelled soap-and-water fresh.

Tom. Why did he have to keep intruding on her thoughts? The deliciousness of Scott's kiss was soured slightly by the thought of him. Slowly, reluctantly, Elizabeth broke the kiss. "Scott, I . . ."

"Shhh. You don't have to say anything, Liz. I know . . . you're pretty confused right now about a lot of things. I just want you to know that I'm here for you."

"Thank you," Elizabeth said simply. She took a deep breath and tried to gather her thoughts. She knew a few things for sure: She knew that she had enjoyed Scott's kiss more than she would have thought possible. She knew that she had some big decisions in front of her, and she knew that she had to talk to Tom. If his memory could interrupt a kiss like the one she and Scott had just shared, then she still had far too much unfinished business with him.

Denise fastened the teardrop choker around her neck. The contrast of the rich red garnet was striking against her navy chiffon dress, and her elegant upswept hair showed off the necklace to perfection. After putting the finishing touches to her makeup and slipping on her new matching heels, Denise stood back and looked at herself in the mirror. There was no denying that the outfit was gorgeous. But a frown marred her pretty face as she realized that there was one problem.

How could she *possibly* be expected to make a decision between the navy chiffon or the peach silk when she took Winston out to dinner that night? Denise hadn't told Winston of her plans yet, but she was sure that he'd be thrilled. After all, who wouldn't want to go out to an exclusive restaurant with a beautiful girl?

Denise turned back to her bed and picked up the peach dress. Her cheerful blue-and-yellow bedspread was completely hidden by the loot she'd hauled that afternoon. Elegant hatboxes and soft tissue paper were everywhere; bright glossy bags tumbled on their sides, spilling out silk scarves and jewelry. Denise looked at it all for a moment and sighed with pleasure.

This is just what I need, she told herself happily. *Right now the only worries I have in the world are whether I can get reservations at La Coupole and which dress I should wear if I do!* As Denise dialed the number of the exclusive French restaurant, she had to pinch herself to make sure that she wasn't dreaming. La Coupole was the kind of place that your parents took you to—for graduation! *Why wait until graduation?* Denise thought as she made reservations for eight o'clock. *Just wait until Winston hears about this!* She quickly punched in his number.

"Winston, guess what!"

"Let me guess . . . you won the lottery."

Almost! "No, silly. I want to take you out for dinner."

"Great," Winston said enthusiastically. "Let's go back to that place with the atomic nachos. We'll split. I want extra jalapenos, extra hot sauce, and extra peppers. I hope you don't mind if we get them without cheese, Denise, because you know I have a sensitive stomach."

"Winnie!" Denise giggled. "I want to take you to La Coupole!"

There was silence on the other end of the phone. "But Denise! Why would I want to go to La Coupole when I could microwave some soup in the dorm?"

"I love you, Winnie." Denise collapsed, laughing, on the bed. The sound of tissue paper crumpling was music to her ears.

"Seriously, what should I wear?" Winston sounded worried.

"Don't worry, Winston. I've got *just* the thing for you!" Denise assured him. She couldn't wait to see how Winston would look in his ascot.

"You're taking me to La Coupole *and* you got me the outfit to wear there too?" Winston asked, incredulous. "What time should I pick you up—that is, if you haven't hired a limo or anything!"

Hmmm, a limo. That's not a bad idea. . . . No, I'll save that for next *week.* "Why don't you meet me here at about seven-fifteen?"

"Sure. Uh . . . Denise? You haven't been drinking or anything, have you?"

"Winnie!" Denise giggled. "I'll see you later!"

Denise hung up the phone, still laughing. Her eyes sparkled as she imagined the evening to come. She pictured the fine china, the elegant service. Nachos? Tonight she'd be dining by candlelight!

No, Denise thought. *Tonight I'll be dining by plastic. Gold card plastic, that is!*

Dana tightened her slender arms around Tom's neck and pulled him down for yet another kiss. Powerless to resist her charms, Tom buried his fingers in the silk of her hair, lowering his mouth to hers one more time.

This is what I should have been doing all along, Tom thought. Dana's kisses were like a drug that blocked out all rational thought. He was dimly aware that the door to his office was open an inch or two, but he was too consumed by Dana's caresses to get up and close it.

A small, startled gasp brought Tom to his senses. "Do you mind knocking?" he asked irritably as he slowly pulled away from Dana's embrace. When he finally looked up to see who had come barging in, Tom groaned. *Elizabeth!*

He stared at her, stunned, unable to move. Her sweet face had never looked more beautiful to him than it did now. She appeared vulnerable and childlike in her baggy overalls, her blond hair loosely pulled back in a ponytail. Tom felt a tug at his heart as he saw how ghostly pale she was. She stood framed in the doorway, one hand on the doorjamb as if she needed it for support. A single crystal tear made its way slowly down her porcelain cheek.

"I . . . I . . . what are you doing here?" Tom demanded. He winced at how harsh his voice sounded. Tom paused for a second to gather his thoughts, but before he could say anything else to Elizabeth, she was gone.

Why did Elizabeth have to show up now? he thought, flustered, as he untangled himself from Dana's grasp. *If only she had come over before! Maybe right now we'd be making up . . . or maybe not. . . .*

Tom's emotions were in turmoil, but Dana didn't seem at all fazed by the interruption. She smiled seductively and reached for Tom, trying to embrace him again.

"Dana, I can't." Tom untwined her arms from around his neck. "It's nothing you've done—it's me. I just can't do this right now." He pushed her gently away. "I need some time alone to think," Tom said quietly. He barely noticed the expression of frustration on her face. Elizabeth's face was the only one that Tom could see. He closed his eyes, trying to erase the image of that tear rolling down her perfect cheek. *What have I done?* Tom moaned silently, burying his head in his hands.

"Well, then, I guess I'll catch up with you later," Dana said, a note of irritation in her voice.

"Yeah, later." Tom avoided her eyes as she straightened out her clothes and gathered her things. Dana acted as if nothing was wrong, but Tom could tell she was trying to salvage her pride. He knew that he was being a heel, but he couldn't seem to help himself. He was in way too much pain to offer Dana anything right now. *I shouldn't have been kissing her to begin with,* he told himself, ashamed. Once again he was just using her in a lame attempt to get over Elizabeth.

Tom sat still for a long time after Dana left, staring at the wall but not seeing anything, his mind a jumble of confused thoughts. He shifted his eyes, and his gaze fell on the copy of *NEWS2US*. Tom reached for it slowly, and it opened right to the page he sought. He didn't even notice Scott as his fingers gently traced the contours of Elizabeth's face. Anyone else looking at the picture would have seen a beautiful girl, but Tom saw far more. She was so dear to him. He cherished her integrity, her spirit, her intelligence.

I miss you so much, Tom thought with a surge of pain. *What happened between us?*

Tom shook his head slowly. He knew what had happened between them, and it was all his fault. *I should have trusted her,* he thought miserably.

But Tom *hadn't* trusted her. His fists clenched as he remembered finding out about George

Conroy's treachery. *I threw away the best girlfriend a guy ever had so I could have a father who turned out to be a snake!*

Tom knew that he'd never be able to forgive himself for what he'd done. "So how could I expect Elizabeth to be able to forgive me?" he asked the empty office. Still, Tom had hoped that Elizabeth *would* forgive him. He'd written her a letter begging for her forgiveness. He had poured out his heart in that letter, *and she never even answered it.*

Holding back tears, Tom walked over to Elizabeth's abandoned desk, remembering how he had considered throwing out the letter. He'd been almost too afraid to send it. What if she didn't answer it? His heart would have been crushed. Tom hadn't thrown it out, though. Instead he'd put it in her in box, and when he came back hours later, the envelope was gone. Yet Elizabeth had never answered.

Why didn't you, Elizabeth? Tom wondered silently. He'd known he was asking for a lot, maybe too much, but he thought that Elizabeth would at least take the time to answer him. He had staked so much on that letter, and she had never even acknowledged it. Didn't she care at all? Did their past relationship mean so little to her?

"We had so much together," Tom murmured, his voice raw with pain. "It's wrong to just throw all that away." A thousand memories of their time together replayed themselves in Tom's mind. He pictured Elizabeth sitting at the desk, her blond hair in a bun held up by a pencil, as she rushed to make a deadline. He remembered being on deadline himself with one particularly important story. He'd been exhausted and starving, too busy to grab a bite to eat. But Elizabeth had surprised him by bringing a picnic basket to the office.

Tom shook his head as he looked at the work-scarred surface of the desk. When Elizabeth had covered it with a red-and-white-checked tablecloth, the room had become more romantic than the finest French restaurant. He tried to picture Elizabeth's golden face laughing, but the image of her crying kept reappearing before his eyes. Tom felt a stab of pain at the vision but also a brief fluttering of hope.

Would Elizabeth have looked so devastated when she walked in on him and Dana if she didn't care anymore?

Tom sprang to his feet and began pacing restlessly, his mind zooming back and forth between the possible explanations of Elizabeth's behavior. But no matter what he came up with, it always came down to one thing.

She never answered the letter, Tom reminded himself as a tear made its way down his face.

Elizabeth ran all the way back to room 28, Dickenson Hall. Her heart pounded and her head throbbed as she tried to push away the awful picture of Dana sitting in Tom's lap. *I won't cry anymore,* Elizabeth promised herself as she pushed open the door of her room and flung herself sobbing on her bed. *I won't!*

Elizabeth rolled over on her back, sniffing as her tears began to subside. "I should have known better than to try and talk to Tom. I *saw* Dana headed there in that ridiculous outfit. . . ." She trailed off and wiped her eyes. "I won't think about it anymore," Elizabeth told herself with determination. "I have more important things to deal with."

Elizabeth got up and headed for her desk. Reaching inside the top drawer, she pulled out the materials from the Denver Center for Investigative Reporting. The glossy brochure and thick course catalog were heavy, but somehow they seemed light as air compared to the skimpy acceptance card.

Elizabeth looked down at the card soberly. There were two boxes that she could check, yes or no. "Just one little black mark, that's all I have to make," Elizabeth murmured. But she knew it was much more than that. Whichever box she marked would affect the next few years of her life—in fact, her entire future.

Pushing the card aside, Elizabeth reached for the course catalog. While SVU had an excellent journalism program with many first-rate teachers,

Elizabeth had to admit that the writing courses offered at DCIR looked more challenging. She nodded to herself as she recognized many of the professors' names. Almost all of them were nationally famous, and she was sure that they would be fascinating instructors. Her heart beat in excitement as she imagined studying her craft under a Pulitzer Prize winner. Could she really deny herself an experience like that? What about the opportunity to be published professionally?

The catalog stated that all undergraduates were given the chance to intern at *real* newspapers and television stations, not just campus chronicles like the *Gazette* or student stations like WSVU.

Elizabeth closed her eyes briefly as she imagined the thrill of working in a real city newsroom or with a professional camera crew. Could she bring herself to turn her back on all those things? *Should* she?

Maybe she wasn't ready for that kind of thing. Maybe she needed more seasoning at SVU first.

Pushing the catalog away with a sigh, she flipped through the brochure. The grounds weren't as lush as SVU's, but the dorms seemed pretty similar. Elizabeth wondered if she could have a single or if she would have to share a room. *Well, at least if I have to share, I know whomever I end up with will be neater than Jessica!* Elizabeth thought with a small smile as she surveyed Jessica's side of the room. As usual it looked as if an entire mall had exploded over there.

She gnawed nervously on the end of her pen. Could she really leave her twin? If she *did* go, missing Jessica would be one of the hardest things she'd have to cope with, if not *the* hardest. Although they'd had their ups and downs over the years, they'd always shared an unbreakable bond. They'd always been inseparable. *What will I do without her?* Elizabeth wondered.

Elizabeth remembered telling Jessica when she and Todd Wilkins had finally decided to go their separate ways. After Elizabeth and Tom had broken up, she had gotten back together with Todd for a short while. But things didn't work out; their ending had been a mutual decision, bittersweet but amicable. Jessica had been shocked that Elizabeth could part from someone she had known her whole life.

But I told her that it didn't matter that Todd and I wouldn't be seeing each other anymore, she reminded herself. *I told Jess that just as long as she never went anywhere, I'd be fine.*

Elizabeth's brow furrowed with guilt as she recalled Jessica's response: "Oh, no problem there. You're stuck with me forever. If I wasn't around, who'd put a little excitement in your life?"

Well, Jessica isn't going anywhere, Elizabeth thought sadly. I'm *the one who's thinking of leaving.*

She pulled the card toward her, her pen hovering uncertainly between the two boxes. "I might

as well just try eenie meenie miney moe!"
Elizabeth cried in frustration, tossing the pen
across the room. It landed in a pile of Jessica's
clothes, sandwiched between a pair of flowered
bike shorts and a hot pink bra.

Elizabeth got up to retrieve her pen. As she
bent down to untangle it from the pink bra an
image of Dana in her leather jeans suddenly
crossed her mind. "Why do I have to keep thinking about Dana?" she moaned. "Correction—why
do I have to keep thinking about Dana and *Tom?*"

Hot tears pricked her eyes once more. Tossing
her head angrily, Elizabeth sat down at her desk.
She stared at the acceptance card for a few seconds
and then with sudden decisiveness started to mark
yes.

"No!" she cried, flinging the pen down again.
"I'm not going to go to Denver just because Tom
Watts hurt me! This isn't about my feelings for
Tom . . . it's about my future *career!*"

Elizabeth gathered all the materials and put
them back in her drawer, closing it with a slam. *I
can't make such an important choice right now,* she
told herself. *I'm just too emotional to make a real
commitment.*

She reached into her closet for a sweater and
stuffed some money and her keys into her pocket.
*I'm going to go on a walk and try and clear my
head,* Elizabeth thought as she opened the door.
After that I'll get something to eat. I'll go to the cof-

162

fee shop and have a salad. No! Forget the coffee shop! I'll go to that new taquería for a burrito.

As Elizabeth headed for the stairwell she smiled for the first time in hours. She had finally made up her mind about *something*.

Chapter Nine

I feel as if I'm a fairy princess—or at least a movie star, Denise thought happily. Her arm rested lightly on Winston's as she glided up the elegant marble staircase leading to the heavy, wrought iron doors of La Coupole. The entrance was flanked by two gilded mirrors; Denise gave each of her reflections a small nod, pleased that she had finally decided to wear the peach dress.

Denise turned to Winston and beamed. She'd never seen him looking as handsome as he did tonight. The striped ascot fit casually into the neckline of his navy cashmere sweater, and his Hawaiian shirt clashed happily underneath. His dark pants flared out perfectly over his new tasseled leather loafers. She gave his arm a small squeeze of excitement and pride.

Winston appeared overwhelmed as he struggled with the door handle. "This place is *incredible,*

Denise. I can't believe you're taking me here."

Before Denise could reply, a valet sprang forward to assist them.

"I guess I haven't been pumping iron as hard as I used to," Winston said self-consciously, fingering his ascot. His face flushed a deep tomato red.

"Oh, Winnie, don't say that." Denise giggled. "You know I love you just the way you are."

"Really?" Winston asked. "I was hoping it was for my gorgeous bod."

"Good evening," the maitre d' announced as Denise and Winston stepped into the gilded entryway. He was dressed impeccably in a black tuxedo. "You must be Ms. Waters and Mr. Egbert. May I show you to your table?"

"Yes, please," Denise breathed.

A hostess appeared and whisked away the spun silver wrap that Denise had bought that afternoon to complement her new silver shoes. Then Denise and Winston followed the maitre d' past a sparkling fountain to a small round table in the corner.

"This is so romantic, Winnie," Denise whispered.

Winston seemed too stunned to reply as he looked around. The gentle strains of a string quartet playing in a corner floated in the air. The waiter appeared at Winston's elbow and handed each of them a large menu bound with a silken cord.

"Say, Winnie . . . do you know what time it is?"

Denise asked mischievously over the edge of her menu.

"Huh? You know my watch is broken," Winston replied. "Besides, who cares what time it is?"

"Well, I thought that *you* might," Denise said casually as she dropped a large beribboned box on Winston's plate.

"Another present!" Winston shrieked gleefully. When several diners turned to stare at his outburst, his eyes widened and he clamped his hand over his mouth.

"Go ahead, open it," Denise urged.

Winston didn't need to be asked twice. He tore off the wrapping, and strips of paper floated through the air like confetti. "A diver's watch! I love it!" he enthused, his voice husky with appreciation. "You're the best girlfriend anyone ever had." He fumbled with the watch as he hastily strapped it to his wrist. "Do you think that I should try it out in the fountain?"

"Gee, Winston, I don't know. Do you think it's deep enough?"

Just as Winston reached across the table to clasp Denise's hands, the waiter approached. "Are you ready to order?" he asked.

"OK," Denise began. "I'll have the beef Wellington and the smoked salmon appetizer, plus the caviar, and maybe some crab cakes too. Oh, and do you have any french fries?"

The waiter raised his eyebrows but didn't say anything.

"Um . . . I guess that's a no. OK, that'll be it, then. And could you bring it all at once? I want to try it all at the same time."

The waiter nodded slightly and turned toward Winston. "And for you, monsieur?"

"Ah, *je voulais l'horloge brûlée avec le cocktail de cravates*," Winston replied.

Denise gazed at him adoringly. "I didn't know your French was so good!"

"Ummm." The waiter cleared his throat. "Let's see . . . you would like a burned clock and a tie cocktail, sir? Or perhaps you meant *l'homard bouillie avec le cocktail de crevettes*? The boiled lobster and the shrimp cocktail?"

"Uh, yeah, I'll have that," Winston mumbled.

"Don't be embarrassed," Denise consoled him. "Anyway, even if you *had* gotten a burned clock, I'm sure it would have been better than anything at the dining hall!"

When the waiter brought out their food, Winston practically began salivating. "This food looks unreal, Denise. I still can't believe you're doing all this for *me*—for us."

"My pleasure, Winnie." Denise loaded her fork with smoked salmon, some caviar, and one of Winston's shrimp.

"Seriously," Winston began between mouthfuls. "Did something happen? I mean, did some wealthy eccentric great-aunt three times removed die and leave you everything?" He waved his arms expansively. "How are you going to pay for all of this?"

"I got a credit card, that's all," Denise replied nonchalantly.

Winston raised his eyebrows and let out a low whistle. "That's really great, but what about when the credit card company sends you *their* bill?"

Denise decided to shut out Winston's last sentence. "Mmmm. This beef is *fantastic*. Do you want to try some?" She forked a large chunk and held it over the table for him to sample.

"Mmmph. Ish delishush," Winston agreed, rolling his eyes in exaggerated delight while he chewed, then gulping loudly. "But I think we should save some room for dessert." He pointed at the enormous pastry cart being wheeled over by the waiter. "How am I going to choose? Everything looks so *scrumpdiddlyumptious.*"

"Don't sweat the little things," Denise told him confidently. She turned to the waiter. "We'll have one of each, and maybe another table too. I don't think that there's enough room on this one."

"Denise!" Winston was shocked.

Denise shrugged playfully and watched in satisfaction as the waiter loaded their table and the one adjacent to it with chocolate mousse, frozen raspberry soufflé, apricot tart, baked Alaska, strawberry shortcake, and éclairs.

Within moments Denise and Winston pushed

aside their half-eaten dinners and dug into dessert.

"This has to be the best meal I've ever eaten in my life," Winston said happily, his face smeared with chocolate.

"Definitely. But I still say that my beef was better than your lobster," Denise insisted as she let a forkful of raspberry soufflé dissolve tantalizingly on her tongue.

Once they'd stuffed themselves silly, Winston excused himself to go to the men's room and Denise signaled for the check. She dropped her gold card on the waiter's little tray and leaned back with a sigh. *Winston and I should make this a regular thing,* Denise thought. *At least every weekend. Maybe more often if we need a special treat. . . .*

"Miss?"

Denise reluctantly pushed aside her thoughts and realized that the maitre d' had just materialized at the table. This time he did *not* look happy. "There's been a small problem," he declared.

"Oh?" Denise raised her eyebrows. "A problem? Well, maybe the lobster was a *little* small, but the beef was terrific." She reached for her water glass to take a small sip.

"I'm sorry, miss, but your card has been *declined*." He dropped the card on the table as if it were covered with a deadly virus. "I'm afraid you'll have to pay cash."

"*C-C-Cash?*" Denise spluttered, spitting out

her water through her nose. "There must be some mistake!"

The maitre d' wiped the front of his tuxedo with a large starched handkerchief. "The mistake may have been on *our* part, Ms. Waters," he said frostily. His face seemed carved from granite. "We're usually more *selective* about whom we allow to dine here. Most people would know better than to order *french fries* with caviar. And, may I say, I found your excessive dessert order *infantile*." He walked away.

"Hey!" Denise called after him, incensed. "I was just being nice before! That lobster was *way* too small!"

Denise angrily avoided the other diners' curious stares. She *couldn't* have been declined. That would mean she'd gone over her limit. It simply wasn't possible to spend that much money in a few days.

Shoving dessert plates out of her way, she began scribbling furiously on the back of the check. *Let's see, the garnet necklace and the silver shoes each cost the same. That's three carry two . . . and the navy dress was . . . umm . . . put down four and carry one . . . then Winnie's gifts, can't forget those . . . and my limit was . . .*

"*Oh,* my *gosh!*"

Winston returned to the table with a large smile on his face. "You should see the bathrooms in this place, Denise. They have *solid gold*—whoa! Is something wrong?"

"Uh . . . Winnie? How good are you at washing dishes?"

"Ouch!" Jessica winced in pain as the heel of Nick's boot ground into the front of her open-toed sandals.

"Sorry—I didn't mean to step on you. I didn't notice where I was walking." Nick gave Jessica's hand a soft squeeze. "I guess I'm a little preoccupied."

In spite of the pain in her foot Jessica had to choke back a smile. *A little* preoccupied? *she thought. Gee, I couldn't tell! If I wasn't holding his hand, Nick would probably have crashed into a tree by now!*

Jessica steered Nick away from a group of joggers and in the direction of Waggoner Hall. From all appearances, it looked like every other Wednesday morning on the SVU campus. But on this particular Wednesday morning the college entrance exams were about to be taken by a gaggle of high-school kids—and Nick Fox.

Jessica took a deep breath of the fresh morning air. It was a typically gorgeous southern California day, and the breeze felt delicious ruffling through her hair. She was sorry that Nick would be shut up in an exam room for most of it.

She looked up at Nick. *I've never seen him look so pale,* Jessica realized. *He could really use some sun.* "Nick? After the test do you want to head over to the beach?"

"Sure, I could take a look at your Jeep."

"*Ni*-ick, wake *up!* I asked you about the *beach,* not about my *car!*" Jessica shook Nick's hand a little. "You know, taking a test isn't a life-or-death thing. You really shouldn't get that worked up over it. At least, *I* never do."

Nick fingered his blue-and-white-striped tie anxiously. "This is important to me, Jess."

Jessica smiled at the picture Nick made in his tie and slightly rumpled white button-down shirt. Jessica had seen Nick in a lot of different looks, from the jeans and motorcycle jacket that he usually wore to the preppy clothes that had been his undercover uniform at Verona Springs. But Jessica had never expected Nick to wear a *tie* today.

Who wears a tie to take a test? she wondered. *That would be like wearing a prom gown to the dentist!* Jessica didn't have the heart to tell Nick that, though. Besides, he looked kind of sweet.

"I'm sure you'll do really well," Jessica said sincerely. She reached over to straighten Nick's tie, which was rapidly becoming unknotted from his constant fussing. *He* should *do well after all the studying he's been doing,* she thought, her mouth curving seductively as she remembered a couple of study breaks they had taken together. *At least I got him unglued from those stupid books every once in a while!*

"I'm really glad you're here for me, Jess," Nick said as they neared the double doors of Waggoner

Hall. "It means a lot to me." His voice cracked when he said *lot*.

Jessica shook her head in wonder. She had been in many different situations with Nick, through hot embraces and flying bullets. She had seen him act with power and strength as he held a roomful of thugs at gunpoint. She had seen him be smooth and subtle, wearing a disguise no one could penetrate. She had seen him be cool and relaxed as he hung out with his friends from the station. But she had *never* seen him be so nervous and awkward, and about something as silly as a *test!*

"Well, here we are," Jessica announced as she slowed to a stop in front of Waggoner Hall.

"Oh yeah." Nick, his forehead glistening with sweat, swallowed hard several times and started to walk inside without even a kiss good-bye.

"Nick, *wait.*" Flashing him a smile, Jessica withdrew a small package tied with a bright red ribbon out of the pocket of her pink linen jacket. "These are for you," she said softly.

"What in the . . . ?" Nick asked as he untied the ribbon. He laughed quietly as he unwrapped two freshly sharpened number-two pencils.

"Just thought they might come in handy."

"Thank you," he said huskily as if Jessica had handed him the keys to a brand-new Porsche. His gorgeous green eyes shone with appreciation as he folded her in his arms and kissed her deeply.

"Good luck," Jessica murmured, touched that

173

her little present had affected Nick so much. "Go on—you better get in there. You don't want to be late." She gave him a playful shove.

Nick nodded and pushed his way through the double doors. He turned back and gave Jessica a weak smile. Then he disappeared into the building.

Jessica pursed her lips. *I've seen Nick leading guys away in handcuffs who looked more relaxed than that,* she thought. With a sigh she settled down on a stone bench to wait for him.

Elizabeth put on her sunglasses as she ducked out of Fairweather Hall and cut diagonally across the quad to the grassy lawn on the other side. She had about twenty minutes before her world history seminar, and she wanted to take advantage of that time to get some fresh air instead of just hurrying across campus. The walk she'd gone on yesterday had helped to clear her head, and she was hoping that this brief jaunt would have the same effect.

Elizabeth smiled as she walked carefully around the sunbathers dotting the lawn, their bright beach towels making cheerful splashes of color. It was hard to be depressed on such a gorgeous day, and Elizabeth found herself feeling more hopeful. Not that she had come to any solution about what to do with her future, but it seemed as if—

"Hey!" Elizabeth's backpack and books went flying as she slammed into a man walking in the opposite direction. "I'm really sorry. It was my fault." Elizabeth bent down to retrieve her scattered belongings.

At least he could apologize too, Elizabeth thought in annoyance. *How rude! Well, since I'm perfectly capable of picking up my own things, he might as well go away. He's making me terribly uncomfortable just standing there.*

The man didn't move an inch as Elizabeth hurriedly stuffed her pens and pencils into her bag. In her rush she brushed against his legs by accident, noting with surprise that he was wearing a business suit. The unexpected contact made her shiver.

What kind of student wears a suit? she wondered.

"Here, let me help you." The man finally spoke. But something about his voice made Elizabeth rear back.

"Don't be afraid," he added, reaching out a hand to steady Elizabeth as she rose to her feet.

Don't be afraid?

Suddenly Elizabeth was overcome with a sickening feeling of revulsion at his touch. She shuddered uncontrollably. Yes, something about this man was familiar—*too* familiar. She whipped off her sunglasses so she could face the man eye-to-eye.

"Mr. Conroy!" The blood drained from Elizabeth's face as she stepped back in shock. Unconsciously she wiped her hands on the front of her jeans. Just looking at Mr. Conroy made her feel violently nauseous. Hot tears of sadness and rage burned Elizabeth's eyes. The pain over her breakup with Tom—a pain that constantly simmered under the surface of her emotions—threatened to erupt with volcanic force. As far as she was concerned, Mr. Conroy was responsible for all the suffering she'd experienced over the past weeks.

I've got to get out of here! Elizabeth thought wildly, but her legs were trembling too much to obey her.

"I was just coming over to see Tom, but I couldn't find him in his dorm or at WSVU," Mr. Conroy said, clearly oblivious to the effect that he was having on Elizabeth. "I was hoping that I would run into you," he continued, dropping his voice intimately.

"Why? So you could come on to me again?" Elizabeth's voice shook with pure hatred. Her legs finally found their strength, and her eyes sparked with loathing for him as she tried to push past.

"Elizabeth—please, wait," Mr. Conroy implored, stepping in front of her to block the way. "I know I must be the last person you want to see, but just give me a chance to say how sorry I am."

The last person I want to see? she thought incredulously. *That doesn't even* begin *to describe the way I feel! He looks repulsive, like something that escaped from the reptile house at the zoo!*

Unfortunately Mr. Conroy seemed to take her

silence as a sign of encouragement. "I feel terrible about what happened between you and Tom, and I know I'm responsible. I couldn't help the way I felt about you. . . . But it was completely inappropriate for me to act on those feelings." He ran a hand through his thinning hair.

"Inappropriate?" Elizabeth asked softly. "It was *insane!*"

"Believe me, I know that—I never wanted—" Mr. Conroy's hands fluttered nervously.

"And worse than that, you told Tom that I was *lying!*" Elizabeth spit out the words venomously. "When he confronted you, you couldn't even come clean. You had to make *me* look like the crazy one! How could you?"

"Please try and understand. . . . I've chastised myself for the way I've behaved countless times. I only hope that things are going better between you and Tom now that he knows the truth." His thin lips twitched nervously in an approximation of a smile.

Elizabeth's heart felt as if it had stopped. "Excuse me?" she whispered, wondering if the shock was making her crazy. "What did you say?"

"I said that I hoped now that Tom knows the truth . . . are you all right?"

Elizabeth's vision began to grow fuzzy, and her knees buckled underneath her as she sank slowly to the ground. The sunshine seemed to turn dark before Elizabeth's eyes, and her head felt as if it were spinning out of control.

I'm just imagining this, she told herself. *This is some horrible nightmare. I'm going to wake up in a minute, and Jess will be in the other bed snoring away—*

"Didn't Tom ever say anything to you?" Mr. Conroy shook his head sorrowfully and knelt down beside Elizabeth. "It's too bad that you haven't patched things up yet."

Elizabeth couldn't bear to look at him for one second longer. Although she felt too weak to move, the desire to be away from him was greater than the nausea that swirled through her stomach. With every ounce of strength she could muster, she staggered to her feet.

"Elizabeth, wait . . ."

Elizabeth paid no attention. She turned and ran. Tears poured down her face as she stumbled blindly into other students. Her body racking with sobs, she pushed past them frantically, not caring where she was going—as long as it was far away from Mr. Conroy. Her mind was blank except for one painful thought that kept hammering inside her head.

Tom knew. He knew!

Ever since Elizabeth and Tom had broken up, only one thing had kept her from completely losing faith that they would ever be able to reconcile things. Deep, deep down, underneath her anger, underneath her hurt, Elizabeth had felt some small spark of sympathy for Tom. Part of her understood that in order for Tom to accept her version of the story, he would have to reject the newfound family that he'd wanted so desperately. Elizabeth could only imagine what it must have been like for Tom, after connecting with his biological father, to have to renounce him. Although Tom had broken her heart, when she peeled away her own layers of pain she could almost understand why he'd done so.

But now that understanding was smashed into a million pieces. Elizabeth would never understand Tom Watts. *He knew!* she repeated to herself. *Tom knew I was telling the truth . . . and he didn't care! He'd rather have a lying, scheming, sleazy, lecherous father than be with me!*

Tears ran down Elizabeth's face as she remembered all the horrible things that Tom had said and done to her since their breakup. *He called me a liar. He* humiliated *me! Why would he behave that way?* Elizabeth gasped as she realized the only possible explanation for Tom's behavior.

"He hates me," she said aloud.

The force of the thought brought her to a standstill just outside Dickenson. "Tom hates me!" Elizabeth clutched her sides. The pain in her heart was so overpowering, she didn't know if she could take another step. She slid down against the side of the building and sat on the grass.

And what about Dana? Elizabeth gasped. *He knows the truth about me—and he's still going out with* her! The memory of Dana in Tom's lap flashed through Elizabeth's mind once again, and she closed her eyes briefly to blot it out. She had hoped—no, *prayed*—that Dana was a phase Tom was going through, someone he was seeing on the rebound.

"But obviously that's not the case." Elizabeth moaned. "He really wants to be with her." The hurt that Elizabeth felt was so extreme that it seemed to burn a path through her soul, leaving only emptiness and hopelessness behind.

I'm so alone, Elizabeth thought, burying her head in her hands. *I used to have brief glimmers of hope that things could work out. Now I have none.*

Maybe Scott was right about Tom, Elizabeth thought grimly. "What did he say? That Tom was a tenth-rate person? It's true! Anyone who could act the way he has . . ."

Elizabeth trailed off as she remembered Tom's vicious attack on Scott on WSVU. Other things that Scott had said about Tom came floating back to her.

". . . this is a personal thing. He's just out to get me. . . ."

"You're right, Scott," Elizabeth said with a catch in her voice. "It *is* a personal thing." Only Tom's attack hadn't been directed at Scott— Elizabeth was sure of that now.

No, she thought. *It was against* me. *Tom hates me so much that he wanted to destroy any chance*

180

of happiness I could find with someone else.

The force of Tom's hatred hit Elizabeth like a blow. "Now I know his true feelings for me," she murmured. "And this is the last time I'm ever going to cry over him. He's not worth it."

She stood up and brushed the grass off her knees. Holding her chin high, she walked toward her history seminar with a purposeful attitude. But she couldn't help thinking how strange it was that although she was determined not to cry, she hurt worse than ever.

Jessica tapped her sandals against the concrete, keeping time with the song she was whistling. She'd been working her way through the entire top forty and was now up to the top three. She leaned back her head and stared up at the sky, thinking how much like cotton candy the powder-puff clouds looked. Today was definitely a beach day, *not* a waiting-outside-for-Nick-to-finish-taking-a-test day. She stopped whistling abruptly and stood up on the stone bench in order to peer into Waggoner's ground-floor lecture hall window.

The room was packed with students frantically scratching down answers as they raced against the clock. Jessica had taken plenty of exams herself and knew what it was like to still be writing when the bell rang. But right now she had no sympathy for the test takers. As far as she was concerned, the bell couldn't ring fast enough.

If Nick doesn't get out of there soon, I'm going to die either of boredom . . . or loneliness . . . or both! Jessica thought with a frustrated sigh. *I'm tired of just hanging out here by myself.* She had spent enough time sitting alone lately to qualify as a Zen master.

C'mon, Nick, she urged him silently, hoping that she could communicate with him telepathically. *Look up here!* Jessica pursed her lips and made a kissy face against the window, but Nick didn't notice. In fact, as far as Jessica could tell, he was staring at his test paper with an even more concentrated expression on his face than any of the other students. *Is he having a hard time?* Jessica wondered.

She watched, fascinated, as he struggled to loosen his tie and then ripped it off as if it had been strangling him. Nick shook his head slightly as if to clear his thoughts, and the gesture made his thick dark hair seem even more wild. The heat in the room must have been intense because Nick unbuttoned the top few buttons of his shirt and rolled up his sleeves.

He's got the most awesome arms, Jessica thought for the thousandth time. His arms were so powerful and masculine. *Just like the rest of him!* she added happily. He looked incredibly hot to her, especially now that he'd lost the tie.

Nick frowned in apparent confusion at the paper in front of him and scratched his stubbly chin. He'd been too busy to shave lately. The sandpaper texture of his jaw as he clenched his teeth in deep thought seemed unbearably sexy, as did his gaunt cheeks. Nick hadn't had much time to eat lately, and the hollowness of his face was a definite turn-on. In Jessica's eyes Nick looked like a slightly wild gypsy.

He should take me in his arms and carry me off across the moors, she thought longingly. *This* was the Nick who drove her wild with desire—this dark, dangerous, edgy guy and *not* the sweet, absentminded professor who he'd been for the last few days. The wave of tenderness that Jessica had felt for *that* guy was fast disappearing. *This* was the Nick she'd fallen in love with.

Jessica remembered how the first time she had seen him at the student center, she had thought that he looked like James Dean. Jessica *loved* James Dean. She wasn't so crazy about the Professor on *Gilligan's Island*.

With a deep, heartfelt sigh Jessica turned away from the window and sat back down on the bench. *I love Nick. I love everything about him. I really do. But I can't help being turned on by his on-the-edge lifestyle. Who wouldn't prefer a guy who wears a motorcycle jacket over a guy who wears a pen protector?*

Jessica nervously pleated the folds of her silk skirt with her hands. Swirls of anxiety rippled through her as she remembered how frightened she'd been at the thought of him hurt and wounded. "I can't go through that again," she murmured, pressing her hand to her stomach. But what could she do?

With a sudden flash of insight Jessica realized just what she *had* to do. She had to stop living vicariously through Nick's adventures. She needed an on-edge lifestyle of her own. With a nostalgic sigh she remembered how much fun she had had going undercover as Perdita. The deadly peril she had experienced on the final night of the investigation, when she had thrown herself from the speeding van into a ditch, had thrilled and invigorated her. The adrenaline high she had felt from the danger only whetted her appetite for more.

"Let's face it," Jessica said to herself with a wry grin. "If my life was that exciting all the time, I wouldn't need Nick's to be!" Jessica knit her brows in a frown as she considered the likelihood of having another experience like the one at Verona Springs. How could she have excitement like that in her life on a *weekly* basis? If she joined the police academy, perhaps?

No, that'd be too dangerous. She'd just experienced the fright of her life, wondering whether or not Nick had gotten hurt on the job. She wasn't willing to go *that* far, was she? Jessica racked her brains, but she couldn't come up with an answer.

"I have to talk to someone," she exclaimed, her voice tinged with urgent need. "Someone who can help me figure out what I should do with my life."

Jessica considered giving Lila a call, but Lila was probably busy with Bruce. Besides, as much as Jessica loved Lila, she wasn't the right person to talk to about this kind of thing. Lila had made it clear that she was getting a little bored hearing about Nick and Jessica's undercover experiences.

No, I need to talk to someone who knows me better than I know myself, she realized. *Someone who cares about my future as much as I do. Someone like Elizabeth!*

Jessica sprang up from the bench and skipped across the quad toward Dickenson Hall, completely forgetting all her anxious, icky thoughts of the past half hour . . . and completely forgetting about Nick.

Chapter
Ten

C'mon, people have been born, grown up, and gotten married in less time than it's taking me to decide yes or no! Elizabeth chastised herself as she sat at her desk and stared down at the acceptance card. It seemed so innocent.

How could such a small thing have such a major impact on my life? she wondered, anxiety creasing her brow. Elizabeth shook her head in frustration. She was determined to make a decision today. *I'm not leaving this room until I do!*

Elizabeth nervously chewed on the cap of her pen. *This shouldn't be such a hard thing to do. I should just make a list of all the pros and cons. Then I'll add them all up, and whichever list is longer . . .*

She tore a sheet of paper out of her notebook and divided it in half. *Well, moving hundreds of miles away from Tom Watts certainly heads the pro list,* Elizabeth thought, blinking back tears.

"Elizabeth!" Jessica burst through the door like a hurricane. "I'm so glad you're here. I really need to talk to you!" She flung herself on her bed, scattering her belongings all over the room.

"What's up, Jess?" Elizabeth asked weakly. She was glad that Jessica wanted to talk; it gave her a legitimate reason to procrastinate. Elizabeth shifted her textbook on Jacobean drama over slightly so that both the acceptance card and the sheet of paper were hidden.

"I don't know what to do, Liz," Jessica wailed. "I just feel so confused!"

"About what?" Elizabeth quirked an eyebrow at her sister, surprised. Although Elizabeth was used to Jessica's emotional outbursts, this time her cry for help seemed more serious in some subtle way. *Jessica looks as if she's hurting,* Elizabeth mused as she regarded her sister silently. *What happened?*

"It's Nick, Elizabeth," Jessica continued.

"Nick? What about Nick?"

"I feel as if I'm going to lose him!" Jessica cried.

"Did you have an argument?"

Jessica shook her head silently.

C'mon, Jess, help me out here, Elizabeth thought, suppressing a smile. It was pretty rare to see Jessica have a hard time spilling the beans. "So . . . did something happen?"

187

"It's just that this whole school thing seems so . . . I don't know. I just feel as if he's pulling away from me somehow," Jessica concluded, near tears. "It's almost as if he's becoming a different person! I mean, I really love Nick, and he used to love me, but now I think he finds the definition of the word *eelymonastery* more interesting than me!"

Eelymonastary? "Do you mean *eleemosynary?*" Elizabeth wrinkled her brow.

"And that's not the only thing," Jessica continued. Now that the story of her plight was under way, the words came tumbling out. "For a while I was glad that Nick wanted to go to school and quit the force. I mean, his job's really dangerous! But I *love* that his job is dangerous. It's so exciting! So then I realized that if I had an exciting job of my own, I wouldn't have to experience excitement through him, right? But what does any of that matter if I lose Nick because he has more fun *studying* than hanging out with me?" Jessica collapsed against her pillows dramatically.

"Whoa!" Elizabeth held up her hand. "I only caught about every other word. Do you mind going over that again? *Slowly?*"

"Nick wants to quit the force," Jessica said with exaggerated slowness. She dried her eyes with the back of her hand and went over to the fridge. "Did you finish all the iced tea, Liz?"

"No . . . there's still a bottle in the back," Elizabeth remarked, watching Jessica root around

188

in the refrigerator. "I don't get it. You told me he was thinking of quitting a few days ago."

"Well, you said to take it *s-l-o-w-l-y.* . . ." Jessica grinned slightly. "How old is this Chinese food?" She sniffed a carton suspiciously. "There's no—oh, here it is." Jessica took out a bottle of iced tea and took a long swallow. "Want some?" She held out the bottle to her sister.

"No, I want you to finish your story," Elizabeth said with a slight touch of impatience.

"OK. Well, I realized I don't want to worry about Nick all the time. After all, police work is dangerous. So I'm kind of glad he wants to quit." Jessica paused for a sip of iced tea. "But now he seems to be getting into school so much! I don't want him to die in a shoot-out, but I don't want to lose him to a bunch of dusty old books either."

"I don't think you have to worry about that." Elizabeth grinned wryly. "In fact, since you *want* Nick to quit, it sounds as if things should work out fine."

"But Elizabeth, don't you see? I love all the excitement of Nick's lifestyle!" Jessica flopped down on her bed, splattering little droplets of tea around. "I *need* that excitement. I can't expect to get it through Nick anymore, so I'll have to go out and find some on my own."

Elizabeth gave Jessica a small smile. She knew that on the outside she looked calm and collected, like the perfect caring adviser, but inside she was a mass of writhing emotions. Visions of Jessica seeking excitement filled her head. Skydiving, bungee jumping, joining the FBI. Which of them would Jessica try on her quest for excitement? As far as Elizabeth was concerned, Jessica had the most exciting life of anyone she knew. If it wasn't enough to satisfy her already, then what would it take?

If I go away, who will stop Jessica from getting mixed up in something crazy? she asked herself. *Who will watch over her if I'm not here? And who knows where this search for excitement will take her? If something happens to her, I'll never forgive myself!*

Elizabeth swallowed hard against the sudden tide of emotion that threatened to engulf her. *I've been so focused on everything else—the courses the journalism program has to offer, getting away from Tom—I haven't* really *let myself dwell on what it would mean for me to leave Jess!*

"You know, Elizabeth, just talking this out with you has made me feel better already." Jessica flashed her sister a lopsided smile. "I mean, I still don't know what to do or anything, but I don't feel as crazy about it as I did ten minutes ago. Sometimes I feel sorry for all the people in the world who don't have a twin."

I feel sorry for all the people in the world who don't have a twin....

190

Elizabeth felt a pang of guilt. *I'm starting to understand how* I'll *feel—but what about Jessica? How will* she *feel if I leave?*

Pushing aside her guilt, she cleared her throat. "Well . . . I'm glad that you're feeling better." With each word the guilt slowly turned like a knife around her stomach. "But I really didn't do anything."

"You didn't have to. Don't you get it? That's the *point.* You helped just by being my sister and by being right here." Jessica jumped up from her bed, unaware of the effects that her innocent comments were having on Elizabeth. She went over to her dresser and began to rummage through the drawers. "Have you been outside today? It's really gorgeous. I'm going to sunbathe on the quad. Do you want to come?" Jessica grabbed a halter and a pair of cutoffs. She pulled off her silk skirt and tossed it on a lamp shade.

"No thanks." Elizabeth could see the corner of the acceptance card sticking out from under her textbook. "I have . . . some things to do."

After Jessica left the room, Elizabeth pulled the acceptance card and the sheet of notebook paper out from under the drama book. *What am I wavering for?* she asked herself. *I can't leave Jess. It's an easy decision.*

She began to check the no box with a forceful stroke of her pen. "No!" Elizabeth cried in frustration. "I can't throw a chance like this away so easily. I can't." She thrust the card away from her and buried her head in her hands with a moan. She thought of how happy Jessica had looked after talking through her problems. *If only my own problems were so easy to get over,* Elizabeth thought with a heavy sigh as she put the card away in her desk.

Denise hesitated on the stone steps that led up to the door of the redbrick bank. The Sweet Valley offices of the Only Bank of Gittenbach, New York, were not particularly large, but to Denise they seemed as imposing as Fort Knox. Still, Denise knew she had to see Andy Newman and take care of her credit problems today or else.

I'd rather have a root canal, Denise thought miserably as she swallowed past the lump in her throat and walked up the rest of the stairs.

A blast of frigid air greeted Denise as the revolving doors spun her inside. She was wearing a simple cotton sundress, and the chill was unpleasant. Denise rubbed the goose bumps on her arms and made her way over to customer service.

"Could you please tell me where I could find Andy Newman?" she asked the clerk behind the desk. The clerk pointed her pen toward a desk in the back.

"Thanks," Denise said nervously. Denise's feet sank into the plush red carpet as she walked toward Andy's desk, but despite the thickness of the carpet one of her shoes squeaked. Everyone turned to stare at her as she made her way through the bank.

"Hi, Andy." The echo of Denise's voice quavered in the air as she stood in front of his desk.

"Do I know you?" Andy looked at her sharply. He was wearing a dark, severely cut suit and a pair of horn-rimmed glasses. His tone wasn't very friendly.

"Uh, we met the other day at SVU?" Denise offered, surprised. She checked the nameplate on his desk again to make sure that this was the same guy. The Andy Newman of a few days ago had been young and laid-back; in his jeans and casual shirt he hadn't looked much different from a student. But this guy seemed much older and much sterner, like an undertaker. He looked like someone who positively enjoyed repossessing old ladies' houses. "I signed up for an SVU gold card, preapproved. Don't you remember?"

"I sign up a lot of students, Ms. . . ."

"Waters, Denise Waters," Denise said. She sat down in the chair in front of Andy's desk. While Andy's chair was upholstered in handsome burgundy leather, Denise's was a plain metal folding one. She shifted uncomfortably. "Um, you signed me up, but I just have this little problem, and I was wondering if something could be done about it," Denise said nervously. She tried to smile at

Andy, but it came out as more of a wince.

"Problem? What kind of problem?" Andy Newman gave her a hard stare.

Doesn't this guy even know how to smile? Denise wondered. "Well, I'm sure we can work it out. I just need a little extension, maybe a couple of months. . . ."

"I'm afraid I don't understand what you're talking about. What do you need an extension *for,* Ms. Waters?" he demanded as he leaned back in his chair and fiddled with his gold pen.

"I, well . . . I was forced to charge over my limit," Denise admitted in a rush.

Andy raised his eyebrows. "Forced?"

"Yes. You see . . ." Denise trailed off, flustered. She didn't think that Andy Newman would be able to appreciate how impossible it was to choose between three equally gorgeous dresses. "I got a little carried away," Denise said, avoiding Andy's eyes. "My card was declined at this really fancy restaurant. I took care of the restaurant bill . . ."

Boy, did I ever, she added silently as she rubbed her hands—which were still chapped from all the dishes she'd had to wash—together anxiously.

". . . but I still have to pay you guys off, so I thought . . . maybe you could give me a little time?"

Andy was silent for a moment. "Ahhh. I see. May I have your card, please?" He reached out his hand.

What's he going to do, rip it up? Denise wondered. Her hand trembled slightly as she handed over the slim gold plastic card. Andy took the card and began to punch numbers into his computer.

"Hmmm . . . well, you certainly *did* buy quite a few things, didn't you?" He sounded almost as if he was impressed by the amount of money that Denise had managed to get through in so short a time.

"It's going to be all right, isn't it?" Denise asked. "I mean, you *will* be able to work something out, won't you? Some kind of payment plan?"

"Oh, we'll be able to make up a payment plan, all right." Something about the way he said it didn't sound very reassuring. "Let's see." Andy began plugging numbers into a fancy jeweled calculator. "First we'll have to raise your interest rate to seventeen percent."

"Seventeen percent?" Denise squealed. Several of the other people in the bank turned to stare at her.

Andy's only reply to her outburst was a raised eyebrow. "Then, because you went over your limit, we'll have to add a penalty. Let's see . . . that seems right." He showed Denise the window display on the calculator.

That's not that bad, Denise thought. *I just won't be able to eat for a couple of weeks.* "So if I pay that, I'll be all square, right?" she asked, hope rising in her voice.

Andy stared at her as if she had suddenly grown two heads. "Oh no. That's just the minimum balance. I'm afraid you're a bad customer now, Denise." He shook his head sorrowfully. "You have to pay *much* more than that."

"How much more?" Denise whispered, feeling slightly faint.

Andy went back to work on his calculator. He seemed to be plugging in an almost infinite number of figures. "Mm-hmm, I think that about covers it," he said finally. Andy showed Denise the numbers flashing on the liquid crystal display.

Denise's heart sank as she regarded the blinking figures. She wasn't feeling faint anymore, but she *was* feeling sick to her stomach.

"I don't *have* that kind of money!" Denise cried in terror. It was true. There was no way she could scare up that kind of cash—she'd never had that much at any given time in her entire life. And Andy Newman expected her to pay that much every *month*? If he had asked her for her firstborn son, she might have rested a little easier.

"You should have thought of that before," Andy chastised sternly. "All I know is that's the amount you owe us. Once a month. And my bosses can be pretty sticky if people don't pay on time."

"But I *can't do it*," she wailed. "It's impossible."

"Then maybe you should borrow it from a friend, Ms. Waters."

"But—but—but *you* said *you* wanted to be my friend," Denise stammered. "Don't you remember?" She pointed at the sign on the wall, bearing the company's logo. "The Only Bank of Gittenbach, New York. *We want to be your friend.*"

Andy's eyes followed Denise's accusing finger. He shrugged and turned back to look at her. "What can I tell you, Ms. Waters? I think you should find yourself some *other* friends."

"Yes!" Nick raised his fist in a victory punch as he walked out through the double doors of Waggoner Hall. He felt sure that he had done well on the exam. Now that the test was over, he could hardly understand why he'd been so nervous. Oh, sure, a couple of the questions had been really challenging, but they hadn't stumped him. Nick was glad that all his studying had paid off, and even though he was bone tired, he couldn't wait to celebrate with Jessica.

"Jessica?" *Where is she?* he wondered, disappointment clouding his face. He looked around but didn't see any sign of his girlfriend. *Maybe she just took a little break,* Nick told himself. *I'll hang out here for a while. She'll show.*

Nick walked over to the bench where he had left Jessica a few hours earlier and sat down. He shoved his crumpled tie in his jacket pocket and rolled up his sleeves as he settled in against the cold stone bench to wait. The test had been exhausting, and Nick was ready to relax. But not without Jessica.

He looked to the left to see if she was coming across the quad and to the right to see if she could be coming from the direction of the student union. But there was no sign of her. Nick felt a flutter of disappointment but continued to wait patiently.

Nick had kept himself going in the exam by taking minibreaks from the test every half hour or so. During those times he energized himself with thoughts of the evening ahead. He and Jessica would order in and rent a romantic movie. Then they'd snuggle up on the couch to watch it. Or maybe Jessica would want to go out to dinner—Nick didn't care. He just wanted to spend some time alone with the woman he loved. The past week of studying had barely left him time for anything else, and now he wanted to make up for it. *But it doesn't look as if I'm going to get the chance*, Nick thought as he checked his watch. *Not if Jess doesn't show up soon.*

He let out a heavy sigh. He was so used to having Jessica around, bubbling with enthusiasm about him and his work. Usually when he came back from a job, she was waiting for him, breathless with impatience, bombarding him with a thousand questions about what had just gone down. And when she was satisfied that she'd heard enough, then she wanted to start kissing. It hadn't taken much for Nick to get used to that kind of homecoming, and he missed it now. Still, he had to admit there was something more exciting in hearing his stories about bringing down a drug ring than how he'd answered the second question on the vocabulary section.

C'mon, pal, aren't you asking a little much? Nick taunted himself as he laughed self-consciously. *You can't ask a girl to wait all breathless and passionate for you to finish taking a* test!

Elizabeth grabbed a turkey sandwich and a small salad and put them on the blue plastic tray. Robotically she picked up a carton of skim milk without even looking as she moved forward on the student union cafeteria line.

As Elizabeth stood at the end of the line waiting to pay for her food she scanned the cafeteria, looking for a good place to sit. The cafeteria was usually full on Thursdays—it was the only day that pizza was served—and there were hardly any free tables.

Elizabeth looked around to see if there was anybody she knew whom she would want to eat with. There was a group of girls from her comparative literature seminar sitting over by the window. The sun streaming on their table made it look very inviting, but Elizabeth didn't feel like sitting with them. Two guys from one of her writing classes were sitting at a table in the corner, hunched over a copy of the *Gazette*. Elizabeth liked them both, but she wasn't in the mood for shoptalk. And over by a small table near the exit, sitting all alone, was Tom.

Elizabeth's heart lurched painfully. She nearly dropped her tray as she stood looking at him. With his back turned to her, she had the luxury of watching him without his knowing.

Tom sat quietly eating his sandwich and reading a book, a cup of coffee by his elbow. He didn't seem to have a care in the world. *He certainly doesn't look like the monster I know him to be,* Elizabeth thought bitterly.

"What should I do?" Elizabeth murmured to herself. Her first instinct was to run. The staggering pain that she had felt yesterday after her fateful encounter with Mr. Conroy was still fresh. Elizabeth didn't know if she could face Tom or even sit in the same room with him.

But I can't just run away, Elizabeth told herself. *I can't keep having every move I make be dictated by Tom Watts. Just because he's eating his lunch here doesn't mean I can't!* Elizabeth moved forward as the line got shorter, realizing as she did so that she only had a minute or so before she would have to make a decision.

"I'm going to walk right by him and sit where he'll be *sure* to see me," Elizabeth murmured with a decisive nod. "I'll act as if *I* don't have a care in the world. I'll show him that *he* doesn't matter to *me*!" Elizabeth felt empowered by her choice, even though her hands shook as they held the tray.

But if you do that you'll be letting him off easy, a voice in Elizabeth's head challenged. *You have to confront him!*

The girl two places ahead of Elizabeth paid for her food, and Elizabeth felt a surge of adrenaline as she realized that after all the failed attempts of the past few days she was finally going to talk to Tom.

Well, maybe yell *is a little more like it,* she thought. Her mouth twisted in a wry grin as she tried to quell the butterflies that were teeming in her stomach.

Elizabeth stiffened as she realized the direction that her anger and pain were taking her. Could she really make a scene in the cafeteria? Scenes were not Elizabeth's style. Maybe she should just forget the whole thing.

But this isn't just about me anymore! Elizabeth told herself. *Tom totally tried to slander Scott, and all because of how much he hates me. I can't let him get away with that!*

Elizabeth squared her shoulders. She might be a little shy about standing up for herself, but not about standing up for her ideals. And as far as she was concerned, Tom had crossed the point of no return. He'd let his feelings about her cloud his journalistic judgment. That broadcast about Scott had been nothing more than a pack of lies fueled by Tom's own personal agenda. *No ethical journalist would do a thing like that,* Elizabeth fumed as she reached the end of the line and paid for her food.

Her heart was pounding as quickly as if she had just run a marathon. She shifted her backpack as she picked up her tray and walked quickly through the length of the cafeteria until she was standing just a few feet behind Tom.

You don't have to do this, she told herself. *You can still just go sit somewhere else and eat your lunch in peace.* But the hurt that burned through Elizabeth gave her the strength to go on. Her pace picked up as she marched the last few feet. She fixed her most determined look on her face as she came to a stop in front of Tom's table.

"Just who do you think you are, Tom Watts?" Elizabeth demanded. Her voice was soft, but her eyes were as hard as flint.

Tom snapped his head up from the book he was reading, his eyes widening in surprise. Elizabeth dropped her tray on the Formica table with a loud clatter. Her food slid off the tray and onto the floor. Lettuce leaves fell to the ground, and milk spilled everywhere. But Elizabeth didn't care. She felt a savage thrill of triumph at the expression of shock on Tom's face. He dropped his own cup of coffee, splattering the hot liquid all over the front of his sweatshirt.

"Elizabeth, what the . . . ," Tom spluttered as he made a grab for a napkin and began mopping up his spilled coffee.

"I *said,* just who do you think you *are,* Tom, and what was that flimsy excuse for a broadcast the other night?" With each word Elizabeth's voice grew in confidence—and decibels. "Were you just trying to hurt Scott? Or did you do it to hurt *me?*" Elizabeth crossed her arms over her chest and stared at Tom defiantly, daring him to respond. "Whatever the reason was, you were *totally* out of line!"

Tom stared at Elizabeth in a complete state of shock. He couldn't believe what he was hearing. Her opening words, spoken in such a soft voice, had confused him. For the tiniest tenth of a second he had thought that she was coming over to make peace with him. His heart had contracted with happiness. But then he had seen the look in her eyes, and chaos had broken out.

Tom dabbed ineffectually at the coffee stains on his sweatshirt. He couldn't care less about the stupid sweatshirt, but the activity gave him a second to gather his thoughts. Was Elizabeth defending that creep Sinclair?

"Elizabeth, I . . . I don't know what you mean," Tom replied lamely. "Did I do it to hurt you?"

Oh no, Elizabeth. That's the last thing I wanted to do. . . .

Tom ran a hand through his hair in frustration.

He was so rattled by Elizabeth's completely un-characteristic outburst that he couldn't think of *what* to say. "I did it *for* you, Elizabeth. I wanted you to see what a phony Scott is."

Elizabeth's face was a mask of cold fury. She put her hands on her hips and glared like Medusa. "Let me get this straight. You're telling me that you did this as some kind of *favor?*"

Tom stared at Elizabeth. Anger vibrated from her every pore, and her voice dripped with scorn. *What's happened to you, Elizabeth?* he wondered. *You used to be so sweet and kind. You seem so bitter. . . . But I guess you have a right after all I've put you through.*

"Answer me!"

Tom shook his head in sorrow. "I didn't want you to get hurt. I thought that you should know—"

Elizabeth burst into laughter. Its sound was so biting and sarcastic, it made Tom flinch. "*You* didn't want *me* to get *hurt?* After all you've done, Tom, that has to be the most *ridiculous* thing I've ever *heard!*"

Tom flushed to the roots of his hair in shame and humiliation. He knew how ironic that state-ment must have sounded coming from him. But that didn't stop what he'd said from being true. Tom *didn't* want Elizabeth to be hurt by Sinclair *or* by his broadcast. Taking a deep breath, Tom tried to remain calm and choose his words care-fully. "I only meant that . . . I thought you should have some idea of the kind of guy you were getting involved with. Scott's nothing but a fake!"

Elizabeth shook her head in apparent disgust. "So *that's* what this is all about—isn't it, Tom? Who I'm 'getting involved with,'" she snarled. "It's a personal thing with you. You just don't want me to be happy with anyone else. So you lashed out at Scott. You thought that by hurting *him* you would hurt *me* more."

"That's not true, Elizabeth!" Tom yelled at the top of his voice. He didn't want to get into a shouting match, but the look on Elizabeth's face was pushing him over the edge. The impact of her words struck him with sudden force.

I was right about Elizabeth's feelings for Sinclair, Tom thought miserably. *Didn't she just say that I was hurting her by hurting him? Sounds like love to me.*

"Oh, give me a—"

"It is *not* a personal thing, Elizabeth."

"Oh no?" Elizabeth raised her voice even louder. "*Please,* Tom, tell me that this wasn't just about your own personal agenda. You're so jealous of Scott personally *and* professionally that you had to drag his name through the mud!" Elizabeth paused for breath. "Well, I'm sorry that you're so threatened by Scott's success that you have to make up lies about him. Maybe he got into DCIR because of *talent,* not because of *connections,* like you insinuated. How low can you get? Don't you have any ethical standards?"

Tom sprang to his feet, knocking over his chair. He towered over Elizabeth. His heart was thumping in his chest so loudly that he could hardly hear himself speak. "I am *not* jealous of Scott's success!" Tom gripped the sides of the table in fury. How could Elizabeth accuse him of envying Scott's journalistic abilities? The guy clearly didn't have any. "It's *Scott's* ethical standards you should be questioning, not mine!"

"*Scott's* ethics aren't the ones under discussion here, Tom. If you *ever* really cared for me, you would *never* have aired a broadcast like that. You did it because—"

"I did it because it was the *truth!*" Tom's voice ripped through the air. "I did it because I'm a responsible journalist and I *care* about the *truth!*"

"Truth?" Elizabeth said. Her voice was barely louder than a whisper. She staggered backward as if Tom's words had physically hit her; her face went white with pain. "Truth? Oh, Tom, the last thing you care about is the truth."

Elizabeth's words sent an icy dagger straight through his heart. He held on to the table for support, afraid that his legs were about to give way underneath him. Of all the terrible accusations that Elizabeth had flung at him, none had affected him as much as what she had just said.

Maybe it isn't what she just said, Tom thought as the expression on Elizabeth's face nearly brought him to tears. *Maybe it's because she's looking at me as if I'm the most despicable man she's ever seen.*

Truth?

Elizabeth gasped as she stared at Tom. He held her gaze, his eye contact steady and unflinching. How could Tom, of all people, look her straight in the eye and tell her that he cared about the truth? Tom *knew* the truth about what had happened with Mr. Conroy—and he had never said anything!

If he cared about honesty so much, she reasoned, *wouldn't he have come to me after his father told him what really happened? Wouldn't he at least have apologized?*

"How can you say a thing like that, Elizabeth?" Tom barked. "How can you say that I don't care about the truth?"

"How can I say a thing like that?" Elizabeth repeated, her eyes widening in disbelief. "Because you have no respect for the truth, Tom," she continued, the words tumbling out of her mouth as if propelled by the most potent anger she had ever felt. "It's obvious that nothing matters less to you. Forget what that says about you as a journalist, Tom. Just think what it says about you as a *person.*"

Elizabeth saw with savage fury that her words had hit home. Tom had turned completely pale as she raged at him. She braced herself, wondering how much further she could go. Ever since she had run into Mr. Conroy, she had been imagining what she would say if she got a chance to confront Tom. Now that she had the opportunity, she wasn't quite sure of how to start.

She took a deep breath to compose her thoughts. "If you really cared about honesty, Tom, then how come—"

"How *dare* you talk to me like that!" Tom exploded angrily. "How *dare* you pass judgment on me! What gives you that right?" Tom pounded on the table with his fists, sending his overturned coffee cup flying. "I can hardly stand to listen to you, you ignorant, self-righteous *witch!*"

Elizabeth recoiled, her eyes filling with tears. She had gone too far. There was nothing she could do to turn back now.

"How could *anybody* stand to listen to you? How could anybody stand to have a relationship with someone as opinionated and judgmental as Elizabeth Wakefield? *Nobody,* that's who." Tom's eyes blazed with fury as he stalked over to her side of the table.

Elizabeth flinched at the raw emotion in his face. There was no doubt in her mind that she had been right about Tom's feelings for her. It wasn't just his awful words, but the look in his eyes as he said them that convinced her.

He hated her. He really, truly hated her.

"As far as I'm concerned, you and Scott *deserve* each other," Tom hissed through teeth clenched in a vicious smile. "In fact, you're both so stubborn and self-satisfied, I'd say you were *made* for each other!" His voice trembled as he said the words.

Elizabeth was momentarily taken aback. She wasn't sure how the conversation had turned to the relationship between her and Scott. She had wanted to confront Tom about what she had learned from his father. How could she get things back on course?

Was it impossible now?

She closed her eyes for a second and rubbed her temples, trying to clear away some of her confusion. She could feel Tom's warm breath on her face as he stood a foot away, looking down on her. His closeness was disconcerting. It rendered her speechless.

"You're so high on Scott?" Tom yelled. "You think that he and that stupid journalism program are so great? Why don't you just *go* with him?"

"I'm seriously considering it!" Elizabeth shouted back. Her desire to confront Tom flew out the window. His relentless anger fueled her own. "I'm seriously considering it," she repeated more quietly, as if stunned by her own words.

Tom didn't reply. His eyes blazed down into Elizabeth's, but she didn't shy away. She held his gaze steadily with her own. They were both silent for a moment.

Suddenly Elizabeth noticed she was being engulfed by a sound other than the roar of Tom's voice. In a matter of seconds—or was it minutes?—she realized it was silence. The quiet was almost as deafening as their raised voices had been moments before.

Elizabeth and Tom both looked around them. Everyone, *everyone* was staring at the two of them. The entire cafeteria sat stunned, listening to every word that had passed between them. People sat as if frozen, with their cups and forks held motionless in midair. Everyone seemed so engrossed by the scene that had played before them, it was almost as if they had turned to waxworks.

Elizabeth's cheeks flamed in embarrassment at the spectacle she had just helped create. *I guess nobody will watch WSVU tonight,* she thought miserably, tears reaching her eyes once more. *Why bother with the news? They just got all the gossip they need right here!*

Chapter Eleven

If only I hadn't bought that last pair of shoes—well, OK, those last three *pairs of shoes,* Denise thought as she trudged tiredly down the street. Her shoulders slumped over dejectedly, and the many bags she was carrying seemed to weigh more with each and every step she took. But it didn't really bother Denise. Nothing really did because nothing could be worse than the letter that was burning a hole in her jeans pocket.

The letter was so crumpled and stained now that it was barely legible, but Denise didn't need to read it again. The words were burned into her brain:

Dear Ms. Waters,

The financial aid office requests that you begin prepaying the interest on your student loans. Due to your recent bad credit rating, we feel justified in demanding . . .

. . . Blah, blah, blah, Denise repeated wearily to herself. *I only had my credit card taken away yesterday. What did they do at the Only Bank? Send out an all-points bulletin?*

But Denise had far more pressing problems to worry about than how the Only Bank had let the financial aid office know about her so quickly. She needed money, and fast. And try as she might, she could think of only one way to come up with some cash—and that was to start returning the things she had bought.

With a heavy heart Denise pushed open the door of one of the small, elegant boutiques that she'd visited earlier. Just a few days ago the store had been warmly inviting, with an intimate air. Now, however, it seemed claustrophobic; the scent of potpourri in the air made Denise want to gag.

"May I help you, miss?" the saleswoman asked with raised eyebrows, taking in the packages that Denise was carrying. *She* hadn't changed at all from the other day. Her hair was pulled back just as tightly, and she was still flicking away specks of imaginary lint.

Denise shivered a little at the woman's frosty tone. Although the saleswoman hadn't been able to intimidate Denise when she had visited the store before, she was certainly succeeding now. She looked Denise up and down, taking in her sneakers and rumpled jeans with a haughty sniff. Denise tried to ignore her as she dumped her bags on the counter, but she was miserably aware of the saleswoman's eyes boring into her. *Why couldn't this have been her day off?* Denise wondered with an inward groan.

"I'd like to return some things I bought the other day." Denise tried to sound confident, but her voice shook a little. *What am I so nervous about?* she asked herself. *People return things all the time!*

The saleswoman shook the silk blouse out of the bag after unwrapping it from the extremely crumpled tissue paper. She held it up to the light to inspect it. Denise tried to act as if she didn't have a care in the world, but her heart was thumping uncomfortably against her ribs, and her brow was starting to sweat. The saleswoman looked at Denise suspiciously and held the blouse up to her nose.

"I'm afraid this blouse has been worn, miss." The saleswoman tossed the wrinkled blouse back at Denise. If her voice had been frosty before, now it was positively glacial.

"Excuse me? *Worn?*" Denise grasped the blouse, her face flaming in humiliation. "I didn't wear it!" she protested with complete

213

honesty. *OK, so maybe I lent it to Izzy. . . . But she only had it on for a few hours when she went to the movies!*

The saleswoman said nothing more to Denise. She ignored her completely and made a slight pressing motion underneath the counter. Suddenly a burly man appeared at Denise's elbow and grabbed it firmly.

"Excuse me?" Denise protested weakly.

"As the manager of this store, I'm afraid I'm going to have to ask you to leave," the man informed her as he guided her toward the door. He looked more like a linebacker than the manager of a women's boutique, but Denise was in no position to judge. Before she knew it, she was outside on the pavement.

Denise considered going back to all the other stores, but she had a strong feeling that she would have the same experience at each of them. Besides, it wasn't as if Denise felt *good* about what she was doing. She felt like a criminal as she tightened her grip on her bags and slunk away from the store.

I guess I'll just take the bus back to SVU, Denise thought disconsolately. *Maybe I can get some kind of part-time job. There must be* something *I could do. . . . Maybe I could be a dishwasher. Winnie and I certainly have enough experience after the other night!*

Denise walked to the bus stop. She was terribly thirsty, but she was afraid to spend any money on a soda. She wasn't even sure she should really be taking the bus. After all, it cost money, but Denise just couldn't face walking the four miles back to campus with all those bags banging her legs.

As Denise plopped down on the bench inside the wind shelter, her eye was caught by a sign with bold red lettering.

Bad Credit? We Can Help, it read.

Denise blinked several times to make sure she wasn't dreaming. When she had convinced herself that the sign wasn't a mirage, she leaned forward eagerly and copied down the number.

Scooping up her packages with renewed energy, she hurried to the nearest pay phone. She deposited a quarter and quickly began punching in the number.

"Yes, may I help you?" a man's voice asked on the other end of the line.

Denise needed no other encouragement. She spilled out her tale of woe.

"I'm sure that I can help you, Denise. My name is Chris Collins, and we at the Farmers' Federal Credit Union would be happy to be your lender." His voice was friendly and assured. "Here's what we can do for you, Denise. The first thing we'll take care of is consolidating your loans. Then we'll refinance them. That will give you some breathing room and extend your buying power. Of course you'll want a cash advance from us right away. . . ."

"Cash advance?" Denise interrupted. This Mr. Collins sounded like the answer to all her prayers.

"Of course. You'll need that right away so that you can take care of this month's payment."

"Oh. Of *course*." Denise nodded, feeling light-years better.

"You do realize, Ms. Waters, that our interest rates are *higher* than those of the Only Bank." Suddenly Mr. Collins sounded slightly less smooth than he had a moment before.

"Oh, sure! No problem." Denise waved her hand as if he could see it. *So they charge more interest—big deal!* she thought happily. *At least I'll be able to take care of all my bills!*

After giving Mr. Collins her address and phone number, she hung up the phone and walked back to the bus stop with a spring in her step. *So I overspent a little before,* she thought. *So what? The important thing is that it's all going to work out. I can keep all my clothes and pay off all my bills thanks to this new credit card.* Denise couldn't resist breaking into a song as she merrily swung her packages, which suddenly seemed light again, back and forth.

"Credit cards are the best invention ever," Denise warbled happily. "What a country! What a world!" Denise settled down with her packages again to wait for the bus. She stopped singing, but she just *couldn't* stop smiling.

Nick gave Jessica a small, intimate smile as he reached across the table to hold her hand. She was looking especially beautiful in a strapless black sheath, with glittering studs in her ears. Nick couldn't take his eyes off her.

Even Nick himself had taken some trouble over his own appearance tonight. He was wearing black pants and a turquoise shirt that Jessica always insisted turned his green eyes into emeralds. Nick felt good, and he was looking forward to the evening with more anticipation than he had felt in quite a while.

Now that his exams were over, he planned to kick back and relax. Nick had been slightly hurt that Jessica hadn't managed to hook up with him the night before. But he wasn't one to hold a grudge, and now that they were finally together, he intended to have a great time.

He had made reservations at one of Jessica's favorite restaurants, Monaco's, an outdoor café overlooking the beach. They were seated outside on the patio. To most of the other patrons the evening must have seemed slightly chilly, so Nick and Jessica had the deck entirely to themselves. The sound of the crashing surf was more perfect than any sound track, and Nick couldn't think of a single detail that wasn't absolutely right. With a satisfied sigh he dug into his appetizer of spicy grilled shrimp.

"So anyway, like I was saying before, some of the questions were pretty challenging." Nick paused and took a sip of his sparkling water. He looked at Jessica expectantly, but she didn't say anything.

"The math really gave me a hard time," he continued, "but I think I pulled through in the end."

Jessica stared out at the sea, nodding blankly.

"Is something wrong with your salad?" Nick asked, noticing that Jessica hadn't taken a single bite of her appetizer.

"Hmmm? Oh no, the salad is fine," Jessica insisted, but she made no move to eat any.

Nick raised his eyebrows but didn't feel it was his place to say anything more. If Jessica didn't feel like eating her appetizer, it was nobody's business but hers. With a shrug he continued. "The verbal section was much easier. I know I aced that part. All that studying really paid off big time. I know I wouldn't have done that well if you hadn't helped give me those vocab quizzes."

Nick paused and smiled appreciatively at Jessica, but she didn't respond. He scratched his head, slightly confused. "Uh . . . the next section of the test was all about . . ."

Jessica sighed loudly. Nick stopped talking and stared at her. Her face looked gorgeous, but she didn't look as if she had heard a word he said. *Well, I know that listening to someone describe an exam isn't the most thrilling thing in the world,* Nick reasoned, the enthusiasm draining from his face. *But she could at least make an effort to look interested!*

The waiter came and removed their appetizers. Nick noticed that Jessica hadn't taken a single bite of her salad and that she didn't even appear to notice her main course was now sitting in front of her.

"Jessica? Are you feeling well?" he asked, concerned. It wasn't like Jessica not to say a single word all evening and not to eat anything either. One of the reasons Nick had made reservations at Monaco's was because Jessica loved their food so much, *especially* the tangy salad dressing.

"Oh, sure, Nick. I feel great," Jessica said unconvincingly. She took a few halfhearted bites of her crabmeat ravioli.

"OK." It didn't seem that way to Nick, but he didn't want to push things. He cut into his Cajun-style steak, wondering if she was angry at him for hogging the conversation. He cleared his throat. "So, how was *your* day, Jessica?"

Silence. Jessica kept staring out at the sea.

"Help me out here, Jess. Was it something I said?" Nick ran a hand through his hair in frustration.

"I'm sorry, Nick." Jessica shook her head slightly. "I didn't hear you. What did you say?"

Even though she smiled, she seemed to be far away.

"I asked you if your entrée was good. I've never had grilled rattlesnake meat before. How does it taste?"

"It's terrific. Would you like some?" Jessica pushed her plate over toward Nick.

"No thanks." Nick would have bet a million dollars that she'd jump ten feet in the air at the mention of rattlesnake meat. He'd gone beyond being concerned; he was now frightened. "Is anything wrong, Jess?" he asked more gently.

"No, I have enough water, thanks."

Obviously Jessica was in her own world right now. Nick could handle her not being in the mood to talk about his test, but she didn't seem to want to talk about whatever was bothering her either.

Sighing, Nick looked at Jessica and then out at the crashing waves. *Beautiful woman, great food, breathtaking scenery. Everything's perfect,* Nick told himself. *So what's wrong with this picture?*

Jessica nodded in answer to Nick's question. *He* did *ask a question, didn't he?* she wondered with a twinge of guilt. Then again, she wasn't even sure that she had nodded in response. It was impossible for Jessica to concentrate on anything Nick was saying tonight. Jessica *wanted* to be attentive to Nick, she really did, but she had

220

too many other things on her mind.

She'd been overjoyed when Nick had offered to take her to Monaco's. She could hardly wait to have a romantic evening with him after all those nights of watching him study.

I wanted everything to be perfect, Jessica thought bittersweetly, remembering how she had spent even more time than usual getting ready. She had put extra effort into her hair and makeup and had looked carefully through her clothes before finally deciding on the black sheath, knowing that Nick found the strapless look very sexy.

Jessica frowned, remembering how she had gone to check her outfit in the full-length mirror that hung in the dorm hall. She had been humming a little tune as she walked carefully on the carpet in her high heels. Jessica was pretty sure that she looked awesome, but she wanted to be absolutely positive.

That's when I heard.

Jessica closed her eyes briefly, remembering how stunned she had felt on hearing the news. She had just decided that the dress looked better with her hair down than in the French twist she was wearing. While she was walking back to her room to change it, Carrie Levine, a bubbly sophomore, had come bouncing along.

"Hey, Jessica, I heard about the showdown in the cafeteria. I guess you're going to miss Elizabeth, huh?"

"Whaaat?"

"Oh yeah," Cindy Taylor had added as she headed toward the showers. "I was there. I think the walls are *still* steaming! If you ask me, Elizabeth should stick with Scott no matter *where* he goes. That guy's a major babe!"

"You're crazy!" Jill Lombard had stepped out into the hallway from her room. "Tom has to be the sweetest, handsomest guy at SVU! There's something too *slick* about Scott."

"Yeah. I think Elizabeth should stay too," Carrie had agreed. "Besides, she *must* still love Tom. Anybody who makes a public scene like that has a lot of unresolved feelings." She had nodded wisely.

Public scene? Elizabeth? Leave SVU?

Was she having a dream?

"Excuse me, but what are you guys talking about?" Jessica had demanded. "What's this about a scene? Who said anything about Elizabeth wanting to leave SVU?" Confusion and anxiety had wrinkled her brow.

The other women had stared at Jessica in surprise.

"You *mean* you didn't *know?*" Jill had squealed.

"Elizabeth threw a tray of food all over Tom in the cafeteria today," Cindy had chimed in.

"I heard she slammed a lemon meringue pie in his face!" Carrie had added excitedly. "Then he yelled that she and Scott were made for each other."

"That's when Elizabeth told Tom that she was going to go away with Scott," Jill had furnished.

"No," Cindy had insisted. "*I* was there. She told Tom *later*. And it wasn't a lemon meringue pie; it was a turkey sandwich."

Jessica didn't wait around to hear *when* Elizabeth had told Tom that she was going with Scott or *what* she had thrown in his face. Jessica didn't care *when* Elizabeth had made her announcement.

It doesn't matter what time she said it, Jessica told herself sorrowfully. *What matters is that she said it at all!*

Jessica had rushed back to the room and closed the door firmly behind her as if by shutting out the girls' conversation, she could erase it. *Could it really be true?* Jessica had asked herself over and over again. *Could Elizabeth really be thinking of going away and leaving me?*

She had dimly remembered Elizabeth telling her something about being accepted to some writing course. *But she didn't say anything about going away!* she'd recalled.

Now, as Jessica sat on the terrace outside Monaco's, she couldn't stop replaying the conversation from the hall in her head. Jessica blinked back tears as she thought of life at SVU without Elizabeth by her side every day. She tried to smile at Nick as he described his test, but she couldn't really focus on what he was saying. All

223

Jessica could think about was whether or not Elizabeth was leaving SVU to go somewhere with Scott.

How could Elizabeth leave SVU—and me too? Jessica asked herself for the thousandth time. *And how could she make such an important decision without talking to* me *about it first?*

Elizabeth held the acceptance card in her hands, turning it over and over. The card was already prestamped; all that it needed in order to be sent was for one of the boxes to be checked. Elizabeth picked up her pen. After days of thinking about little else besides whether to go or not, she had finally come to a decision.

Elizabeth took a deep breath, then with a sudden decisive motion she started to place a check mark in the yes box.

The phone rang. *Saved by the bell!* Elizabeth thought, grinning wryly. There was nobody she wanted to talk to right now, so she let the machine pick up.

"Elizabeth." Tom's voice filled the silence of the little room with its deep rich tones. Elizabeth closed her eyes and let his voice wash over her. "I just wanted to tell you that I'm really, really sorry about what happened earlier." He sounded a little strained. "I . . . I didn't want to make a scene. I just . . . I only wanted . . . look, I'll . . . I'll be seeing you around, or maybe not. . . . Take care."

The room seemed emptier after Tom had hung up. Elizabeth stared at the little red blinking light on the machine while she thought about what Tom had said. What did it mean? His voice had cracked a little when he said that he was sorry.

Had he been crying? Elizabeth wondered. She rested her chin in her palm. *What was he going to say when he stopped himself? "Elizabeth, I only wanted . . ."* to what? *To apologize? To get back together again? To put this whole mess behind us?*

Elizabeth's heart somersaulted as she considered each possibility. "What about the way he said good-bye," she muttered as she replayed his last words in her head. *I'll be seeing you around, or maybe not. . . .* "What was the *maybe not* about? Did he mean that he thought I was leaving? Or that he didn't care whether I did or not?"

Would he have bothered to call me if he didn't still care? Elizabeth asked herself. She knew Tom's voice so intimately, she was sure that she could understand all its nuances. Tom's voice as it cracked over the words didn't sound like the voice of a man who hated her. It had *sounded* like he cared, almost more than he wanted to admit.

Elizabeth picked up her pen. She hesitated for the briefest of seconds and then began to mark the no box.

The phone rang again. Elizabeth put down her

pen with a frustrated sigh. Once again she let the machine take the call.

"Hey, Elizabeth, Scott here. I just wanted to say good night. Look . . . I want you to know that whatever decision you make about the program, I'll respect it. I respect *you*, Elizabeth, as a journalist and as a woman. . . . Give me a call. Bye."

The machine clicked off. Elizabeth walked over to it and pressed the replay button. Scott's words floated through the room. Elizabeth couldn't read the subtle undertones in Scott's voice the way she thought she could with Tom's, but one of Scott's words seemed to hang in the air even after the message finished replaying.

Respect. Elizabeth tossed her pen on the desk and began to pace restlessly back and forth. *Does Scott really respect me? If he did, wouldn't he have been more upset about the article in* NEWS2US? Elizabeth shook her head slightly, remembering. *No, Scott* was *upset for me.* She recalled how she had never seen him so embarrassed before. Did that mean that *he* respected her?

What about Tom? Did he really have such high regard for her? Did his actions seem as if he *respected* her as a woman and as a journalist? "Oh, what does it matter?" Elizabeth cried in frustration, flopping down on her bed. "The important thing isn't whether Scott or Tom respects me but whether I respect myself." Elizabeth rolled over on her stomach, clutching her pillow to her chest.

She knew that in many ways, transferring to DCIR would be difficult. The courses would probably be much more advanced than those she was used to. But it would be such a *challenge*. The idea both thrilled and intimidated her.

"Could I respect *myself* if I turned down a challenge like that?" Elizabeth asked the empty room. She sat up and threw her pillow over onto Jessica's bed. If she went to Denver, was she giving herself a fresh start, a way to begin again after all her heartache with Tom?

Or am I just running away from it all?

Elizabeth wasn't sure which was the right answer, but if she *was* running away, she wouldn't feel very proud of herself.

And what about Jess? Elizabeth walked over to her sister's bed to retrieve her pillow. *Can I respect myself if I leave Jess all alone? How will she get along without me? How will I get along without her?*

Elizabeth walked over to the window and looked out over the campus without really seeing it. She thought back over the past eighteen years that she had spent growing up side by side with Jessica. Except for a few weeks here and there, they had never really been apart. Could they both handle being separated? Would it be too painful?

Or would it be the best thing for both of us? Would it force us to become more independent?

Elizabeth went back to her desk and stood looking down at the unmarked card. It looked so innocent—just a plain white card. But whatever mark she made on it would have so much influence, not just on her life but on the lives of those around her as well.

Elizabeth picked up her pen one last time and then finally, decisively made her mark. She picked up the card and walked to the door. The sooner she mailed it, the better.

Pausing with her hand on the doorknob, she turned around and took a long look at the dorm room that had been her home since coming to SVU. Her gaze slid over her pink-and-white bed, past the tangle of Jessica's clothes that littered her half of the floor. Her eyes roamed over the walls, past the bookshelves filled with her many books and stuffed haphazardly with some of Jessica's CDs. She saw the picture of their family that hung above her desk and the SVU pennant that was slightly askew above Jessica's.

Elizabeth smiled slightly, her hand tightening on the card as she took everything in. She gave a last look at the room before shutting the door. *Yes.* Elizabeth nodded to herself. *I've made the right decision.*

Elizabeth went downstairs to mail her answer. A warm breeze ruffled her hair as she walked across the quad, clutching the card. Quickly, before she could change her mind, she lifted the

228

metal lid of the mailbox and dropped it inside.

Elizabeth has finally made her decision—and it's too late for her to turn back now. Did she choose to stay or leave? Find out in Sweet Valley University #37, **BREAKING AWAY.**

SIGN UP FOR THE
SWEET VALLEY HIGH®
FAN CLUB!

Hey, girls! Get all the gossip on Sweet
Valley High's® most popular teenagers
when you join our fantastic Fan Club!
As a member, you'll get all of this really
cool stuff:

- Membership Card with your own
  personal Fan Club ID number
- A Sweet Valley High® Secret
  Treasure Box
- Sweet Valley High® Stationery
- Official Fan Club Pencil (for secret
  note writing!)
- Three Bookmarks
- A "Members Only" Door Hanger
- Two Skeins of J. & P. Coats® Embroidery
  Floss with flower barrette instruction
  leaflet
- Two editions of *The Oracle* newsletter
- Plus exclusive Sweet Valley High®
  product offers, special savings,
  contests, and much more!

Be the first to find out what Jessica & Elizabeth Wakefield are up to by joining the
Sweet Valley High® Fan Club for the one-year membership fee of only $6.25 each
for U.S. residents, $8.25 for Canadian residents (U.S. currency). Includes shipping
& handling.

Send a check or money order (do not send cash) made payable to "Sweet Valley
High® Fan Club" along with this form to:

SWEET VALLEY HIGH® FAN CLUB, BOX 3919-B, SCHAUMBURG, IL 60168-3919

NAME_____
                              (Please print clearly)

ADDRESS_____

CITY_____ STATE _____ ZIP_____
                                                        (Required)

AGE _____ BIRTHDAY_____ /_____ /_____

Offer good while supplies last. Allow 6-8 weeks after check clearance for delivery. Addresses without ZIP
codes cannot be honored. Offer good in USA & Canada only. Void where prohibited by law.
©1993 by Francine Pascal   LCI-1383-123

You'll always remember your first love.

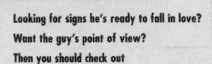
Love Stories

Looking for signs he's ready to fall in love?
Want the guy's point of view?
Then you should check out
the **Love Stories** series.
Romantic stories
that tell it like it is—
why he doesn't call,
how to ask him out,
when to say
good-bye.

The **Love Stories**
series is available
at a bookstore
near you.

BFYR 135

WAKE COUNTY PUBLIC LIBRARIES
4020 CARYA DRIVE

MAR - 9 1998

RALEIGH, NC 27610
(919) 250-1200